"VAMPIRES. OF THE VERY DAMAGED KIND. AW, SOMEONE TOOK ALL THE FUN OUT OF MY JOB."

Buffy stalked forward, stake in hand. The nearest body stirred at her approach, but was unable to do more than glare at her. There were maybe a dozen bodies, half-covered in the sludge that ran along the tunnel floor. All of them lay face-up, huge gouges on their bodies—

Like a shark took chunks out of them, Buffy thought uneasily. It was a Slayer's buffet: Downed vamps, no waiting. But Buffy didn't feel the usual rush of energy that came when given the chance to take out a bunch of demons.

"Looks like whoever—or whatever—it was has long gone," Angel said. He gestured at the watery sludge at their feet. "Washed away any evidence."

"No, not all," Buffy said. She bent, holding her breath, and scooped up something slimy from where it had wrapped around her boot.

"Seaweed," Angel said dismissively.

"In the sewer? This far in? I don't think so." She looked more closely, running it through her fingers. "Angel, this is hair." Holding it up to what light there was, she added, "Extremely green hair."

Buffy the Vampire Slayer™

Available from ARCHWAY Paperbacks and POCKET PULSE

Buffy the Vampire Slayer adult books

Available from POCKET BOOKS

BUFFY THE VAMPIRE SLAYER™

DEEP WATER

Laura Anne Gilman and Josepha Sherman

An original novel based on the hit TV series created by Joss Whedon

POCKET PULSE

New York   London   Toronto   Sydney   Singapore

This book is a work of fiction. Names, characters, places and incidents are products of the author's imagination or are used fictitiously. Any resemblance to actual events or locales or persons, living or dead, is entirely coincidental.

An *Original* Publication of POCKET BOOKS

 POCKET PULSE, published by
Pocket Books, a division of Simon & Schuster Inc.
1230 Avenue of the Americas, New York, NY 10020

ISBN: 0-671-03919-9

First Pocket Pulse printing February 2000

10   9   8   7   6   5   4   3   2   1

Printed in the U.S.A.

Laura Anne would like to dedicate this book to: Jen Heddle, who *still* hasn't threatened to quit, and Lisa Clancy, who wouldn't let *us* quit before we were done.

Josepha would like to dedicate this book to: Joss, the *Buffy* cast, and Lisa the Longsuffering for allowing us another trip into Buffyland, and to the members of #gasp for putting up with the never-ending search for the elusive meerkat.

ACKNOWLEDGMENTS

LAG would like to thank Lynn Flewelling, Dave Logsdon, Sue Gilman, Karen Topinka and the rest of the Electronic Beta Readers Brigade. The stuff we got right is thanks to them, mistakes are the fault only of the authors. And, again, thanks and gratitude to the cast and crew of *BtVS* for doing what they do, so well.

DEEP WATER

CHAPTER 1

The water was all around her, blue-green, murky and cold. At first, it was like watching a movie, some TV show of drowning people, their air bubbles flowing up past the camera lens in a decorative pattern. But then she tried to take a breath, and the water flooded her lungs, seared her brain, and cold, webby hands grabbed hold of her, dragging her down, pulling her away from the air, away from life . . .

Buffy Summers woke up with a desperate gasp, and found herself already out of bed, standing barefoot on the chilly floor. Her nightshirt was soaked in cold sweat, and her hair was stringy, like she'd gone to bed after a shower without combing it out first. For a moment she merely sucked oxygen into her lungs, her chest heaving, thankful for the crisp dryness of the winter air.

"Okay," she said to herself. "That was deeply unpleasant."

For all the perks of being the Slayer, the one who stood between humanity and the nether world of demons and things that went *snarl* in the night, there were times when it really, really sucked. Which was not an expression she used lightly, here in the vampire central that was Sunnydale. Three times in the past month she'd had the same dream. Always cold water, always drowning . . .

Yesterday, she'd finally gone to Giles for advice. . . .

"Don't tell me I'm overreacting!" Buffy stood looking over Rupert Giles's shoulder as he consulted his books. Good old Giles, her tweedy but ever-dependable Watcher—who wasn't being very helpful.

"Perhaps overreacting was the incorrect word," he admitted, looking up at her and pushing his glasses back up on his nose. "But I would emphasize that there seems to be nothing immediate to worry about." Closing the last of the books, he concluded firmly, "There are certain parameters which are used to identify omens or, ah, precognitive dreams. Perhaps you might consider learning them yourself, to ease your concerns."

"Right. In my copious spare time." She chewed on a nail, then realized what she was doing and firmly moved her hand away. "It couldn't be a prophecy, or anything? Something I'm wigging to before you?"

"That was the first thing I checked," Giles said. "While we may have a rather busy spring, there are no prophecies forthcoming which might be suggestive of water, or water-based threats."

"That's it? Just glance at a book and say 'nothing to worry you'?"

"Buffy, even the Slayer can have something as mundane as a nightmare." He stood up, indicating that the conversation was over.

Buffy glared at him, resenting that really irritating combination of sympathy and superiority he got in his voice sometimes.

"Perhaps," he continued, relenting a little under the weight of that glare, "these dreams stem from your string of unpleasant experiences with water?"

"Gee, took all your how many degrees to figure that out?" She felt all the air go out of her then, hearing the bite in her own voice. "No, forget that. Sorry. Unfair."

Giles was her Watcher—her coach, her mentor, her partner—and he knew her probably better than anyone else. But he couldn't read her mind. She had told him—loudly, she recalled now—that she was over the whole being drowned thing. As for the idea of the former swim team maybe still lurking off the coast somewhere—not his fault if her subconscious wasn't as convinced as the rest of her that that was old, done news.

So calm down, Summers. Maybe he's right. Maybe you're just stressing. You've had bad dreams before, and nobody died.

"So you're saying I'm, what, projecting unfinished stuff into my dreams in a perfectly normal ordinary way?"

"So it would seem."

"Great." She pouted. "Gotta tell you, not the way I wanted to be ordinary." *Yeah. Giles is probably right. No, he is right. That's his job, to know stuff like this. So let it go, Buffy.*

Doing her best to shrug the whole thing off, she picked up her books and got ready to head for class.

"Serves me right for saying I was getting bored with the same old, same old vamps."

" 'Be careful what you wish for,' " Giles agreed, moving around her to replace the books on the shelf. "The sleeping mind can play some nasty tricks."

"The sleeping mind," Buffy had corrected flatly, "is a pain."

But that had been then, and this was now. And right now, in the dim faint light that wasn't quite morning yet, something deep in her back brain kept suggesting that Giles was wrong. That there was something more happening with this dream than repressed anxiety.

"Stop. No thinking. Thinking leads to obsessing, and obsessing leads to worse dreams, and worse dreams leads you to the nice white padded room."

Proud of her Psychology 101 evaluation, Buffy replaced her nightshirt with a dry one, and crawled back into bed. Unwilling to go back to sleep, she turned on the radio and, needing to hear a voice other than her own, cruised the stations until she came to a newscast.

". . . reports coming in are that the *Roxanne*'s leak, while significant, will not cause the damage at first feared. The company spokesperson issued a statement stating that crews were able to contain most of the oil within hours of the incident. However, environmental groups are already picketing the ship's owners, Sea-Rac Shipping, for alleged abuses in their safety record. And rescue teams are mobilizing to do what they can for the oil-soaked birds and animals which are being washed ashore. A spokesperson for the Sierra Club says . . ."

Great, Buffy thought. *I spend my nights saving the*

*world, and meanwhile the rest of the human race gets
their kicks dumping in it.*

The sun was rising slowly behind them, catching
glints off the water. The small, curved strip of beach
wasn't likely to appeal to even the hardiest of sun-
bathers, being lined with weather-beaten rocks the size
of large dogs, and strewn with splintered driftwood and
the occasional piles of dried-out seaweed. But the
dozen or so figures walking down the damp sand
weren't there for the sun or the surf.

They had been there for several hours already,
dressed in bright yellow windbreakers and jeans. Some
carried packs, while others played high-powered flash-
lights over the sand, covering, as they walked, the area
still night-shadowed, from the rocks along the road
down to the waterline.

It was slow, nerve-wracking work, with only the occasional reward.

"Here's one!"

The call came from farther down the beach, and Willow Rosenberg hurried to join the speaker; she was one
of those carrying a bundle, and her hands, clumsy in
their protective gloves, busily unwrapped the thick, dry
cloth, which she handed to her companion when she
reached him.

Hopefully, this would be one of those rewarding finds.

"Oh, the poor thing!" Willow crooned, looking over
the speaker's shoulder as he knelt in the sand. In front
of him, flopping weakly, was a large, sharp-beaked
bird, a herring gull, Willow thought, its normally white
and gray feathers now coated with a heavy dark crud,
the result of an oil spill off the coast the night before.

But it was alive.

"Think he'll make it, Sean?" she asked.

"Yeah, I think he's gonna be fine," the rescue worker reassured her. "I'll take him back to the truck," he continued, expertly immobilizing the bird with the blanket and blotting off some of the oil as he did so. "You go on, see if you spot any more. But remember, don't touch them! Call, and wait for me to come."

"Got it," the redhead said, watching as Sean, a solid, competent figure in his windbreaker and matching baseball cap, cradled the bird as carefully as he could, and headed back to the road, where a large van with MARINE WILDLIFE RESCUE stenciled on its side waited to receive his bundle.

"Poor thing," Willow said again, and turned to scan down the length of California coast. She winced at the sight of the pearlized sand now dulled by the same goo which had coated the dozen or so birds they had already rescued that morning. A media truck had cruised by earlier, but the slow search-and-retrieve activity didn't make for newsworthy soundbites, and so they'd moved down the road, looking for something splashier to film. Oil spills really just weren't a story anymore.

Sighing, Willow trudged forward. *If I ever get my hands on whoever did this, I'll—I'll turn them into frogs and drop them into a sewer. See how they like getting slimed, and not being able to breathe!*

A lot of the birds they had found that morning had died before the rescue crews could do anything. The sight of those still bodies, so fragile, had made her madder than she could remember being in a long time. And what made it worse was there wasn't really anything they could do about the people who caused the spill. Lawyers would fight it out, and it would take years, and meanwhile all they could do was clean up the mess.

But that one is alive, she reminded herself. *A lot of them are going to live, 'cause we were here.*

A nagging voice at the back of her mind that sounded a lot like her mother was telling her this was a school day, and she wasn't going to be much good at any of it without at least a little sleep. But Willow closed her mental ears to that voice in a way she wouldn't have been able to just a few years ago. B.B. Before Buffy.

Saving lives, any sort, was kind of more important. Even if they were only animals. Besides, there weren't any tests today. She could catch a nap in the library at lunch, and she'd be fine. No worse than staying up all night to study. Or save the world.

A sudden little whimper made her turn her attention from the shoreline to the tumble of larger rocks behind her.

"Huh." Willow scrunched her face up in a frown. A bird didn't make that kind of sound. But it wasn't just birds they were supposed to be looking for. A seal, trying to get away from the source of the oil? They had been told to especially keep an eye out for some harbor seals that had been sighted in the area earlier, but . . . wouldn't someone have seen it already?

There was another whimpering noise, quickly cut off, and Willow looked around, trying to figure out exactly where the sound had come from.

Over there, Willow decided all at once, then stopped. What had suddenly drawn her attention to that specific area? The sound hadn't been loud enough to be certain . . . but something was prickling at the back of her head, like the feeling she got sometimes when a spell was going to really, really work. She'd learned over the past year or so to listen to that magic-y tingle.

Only remember, Willow cautioned herself. *Just because you're outside Sunnydale city limits doesn't mean it can't be something bad . . .*

Thankful for the heavy gloves she was wearing, not to mention the vial of holy water carried in the fanny-pack cinched around her waist, Willow climbed up over the largest rock, searching carefully for the source of the whimper.

"Where are you?" she asked softly, trying to project warmth and caring into her voice. "Poor thing, I won't hurt you. Come on, let me see you. I'm here to help—"

Her voice caught in her throat, and her eyes widened in shock.

"Oh. Oh wow!"

The young girl, her hair a sleek, dark, wet cap, was naked but for a thin brown blanket of some kind wrapped around her. She was a sturdy little thing, but gave the impression, somehow, of being weak and lost.

Scared, Willow thought. *The poor thing's scared. I'm scaring her?*

The girl stared up at Willow with enormous, frightened dark eyes, then tried to shift away, only to let out a mew of pain.

"Oh!" Her paralysis broken, Willow scooted down the rock, coming closer to the injured girl. "Are you okay? I can help. How did you get caught in here? Did you fall? And what happened to your clothes?"

The girl merely whimpered, trying to push up against the rough rock behind her, as though it would give her some protection against the approaching stranger.

"Hey. You don't have to be scared of me. I'm just trying to help!" Willow stopped, confused and not a little offended. "My name's Willow. What's yours?"

The brown-eyed girl stared up at her, unblinking, and closed her fingers more tightly around the blanket. *Did she understand me?* Willow wondered. *Is she where the tingle came from?*

She crouched by the younger girl, reaching out one hand slowly, the way one would to a strange dog. But when her fingers touched the blanket, Willow stopped, shocked by the sleek feel of it under her fingers. A tingle, yes, stronger than before. But, more, too.

It's not cloth. What is it? Skin. Warm, slick skin. Like suede. But it feels kinda weird, too. Like it's covered in . . . oil.

"Oh," Willow said in sudden realization. "Oh boy!"

CHAPTER 2

"Again."

The voice was British, male, and exhausted. Giles, natch. Willow tugged on the hand of the strange, silent little girl accompanying her, and pushed through the swinging doors. *When in doubt, go to the library.* It was, she thought with a silent giggle, the Slayerette creed, whether dealing with the undead, the monstrous, or the merely freaky.

The rhythmic thudding and thwacking coming from inside the library were familiar sounds: the Slayer in the middle of her early morning workout, otherwise known as beating up on her Watcher.

She so gets the whole "runner's high" thing, Willow thought admiringly, watching the Slayer land kick after kick squarely on the padded target Giles was holding for her. He staggered back after each blow, but determinedly came back for more. Buffy's face was shiny with sweat, but she was grinning with each kick, her whole body alive with energy. *Guess it's a perk you get, whomping on vamps for a living.*

But then Willow saw Oz, sitting at the long table eating his usual post-werewolfy breakfast of Cheerios, dry, and a six-pack of Egg McMuffins, and felt her own little rush of happy as he looked up and saw her standing there. A smile lit his face, and she beamed at him in return.

The little girl stared at Oz, then returned her worried gaze to Willow, as though expecting her to make some sense of this strange new scene. The trip back from the beach, wrapped in the yellow windbreaker and perched double on Willow's bicycle, seemed to have taken care of the girl's hesitation about her rescuer, based on the way she had snuggled against the older girl for comfort. But new people were still something to be cautious about.

"It's okay," Willow said soothingly. "These are my friends."

Buffy, being the Slayer, was already aware that someone had entered the library, and was also aware that it was neither a vampire, because of it being daylight, nor Snyder, because he was off at some principals' conference up in L.A. for the rest of the week. So she took her time, following through with one last kick, then turned and looked toward the door, hands coming to rest on her hips. She took Will in with a smile, then both she and Giles became alert at the sight of Willow's companion. Exchanging startled glances, they started forward, curious, but cautious.

"Hey, guys," Willow said with forced cheer, barely keeping her companion from bolting out the door. "Got a minute?"

* * *

By the time Xander arrived, the little girl had been calmed down, redressed in an oversized shirt and a pair of cut-off sweatpants pulled from Willow's gym locker, and seated in one of the library chairs where she now huddled, clearly overwhelmed by everything around her. The brown sealskin she clutched between oddly delicate fingers seemed to be the only thing that kept her from dying of fear on the spot, like it was some kind of weird security blanket.

"So what with the tingle of magic, and the skin, and, you know, the oil," Willow was saying to Giles, "I thought, probably she's not human, right? Why else would she be there, unless she got caught in the spill somehow, which a person wouldn't have. And I couldn't leave her there—and I couldn't take her to the truck, 'cause well, that would be bad. So I brought her here. So we could figure out what to do." She paused. "What *do* we do?"

Buffy glanced at Giles. He, Sunnydale's resident capital-E Expert on things weird, seemed to be following Willow's narrative, but the others in the library weren't doing so well.

Buffy waved a hand in front of Willow's face, getting her attention long enough for some clarification.

"You're saying that she's some kind of sea-creature whatsis?"

But it was the Watcher who responded. "I believe, based on Willow's observations, that she may be a selkie."

"Silky?" Xander asked in confusion. "I mean, her skin looks smooth, but—"

"S-e-l-k-i-e," Giles corrected. "A natural creature of the sea, a shapeshifter. She may look perfectly human without that sealskin coat, but she is not."

Willow nodded, her eyes lighting up with excitement. "That was what I was thinking. Only, not having run into any selkies—I mean, that I knew about—I didn't know for sure. . . ."

"Breathe, Will," Xander suggested. "Easier to talk that way."

"It must have been the skin," Willow went on, ignoring him completely. "The magic I felt, I mean. The skin lets her turn into a seal, to live in the ocean."

Giles nodded. "Fascinating, really. Selkies are normally found off the coasts of Ireland and most of the other Celtic islands." He stopped to look at their silent guest, his expression thoughtful. "Although I suppose it's not so surprising that they would live along this coast as well, with its rather varied marine population."

"Yeah," Willow said. "There's a huge harbor seal population along the coast, all the way down to Mexico. Maybe her folk live with them, or are neighbors, or something."

"Cool," Oz said, nodding along with Willow's logic.

"Okay," Buffy said quickly, before either Giles or Willow could start going into informational overload, "that's enough of a Nature Moment for me. So what you're saying is, sometimes she's a seal. Except when she's not." She shrugged, relieved to have it solved so simply. "Not a vampire, not out to maim and destroy—not my problem. Shapechanging, human to animal . . . Oz, I think this is more your department."

"Oh, goodie," Xander said with fake cheer from where he was sprawled in a chair, his long legs stretched out under the table, across from Oz and Willow, who were sharing a chair and what was left of

Oz's breakfast. "Two shapechangers for the price of one. What is this, the Hellmouth Zoo?"

"Xander!" Willow said indignantly.

"Technically," Giles cut in, "a selkie is not a were creature, not in the traditional sense, at least. 'Were' means 'man,' and refers to a human who takes on another form. The selkie's natural form is that of a seal. It is only when they, ah, remove their skin that they take on human form."

Buffy shrugged. "So why don't we just zip her back up into her pelt, and send her on her way?"

" Because it's all covered with oil," Willow explained. "I tried to get the goo off, the way they showed us, but it won't go. And I'm scared I'm going to hurt it or its magick or something if I scrub it. And besides, every time I try to get her to let go of the skin altogether, she curls up in this tight little ball and I feel like I'm hurting a puppy!"

Giles took off his glasses, folded them, and tapped them thoughtfully against his other hand. "Yes, of course she'd be terrified of losing the skin. There are folk tales of selkies trapped on land in human form when their skins are stolen. Stolen by humans, I might add. Doubtless such tales are told among her people, as well.

"As for the 'goo,' as you call it, I suspect that normal cleansing methods would not work on something with such a strong magickal aspect. . . ."

Buffy straightened, suddenly remembering the really weird thing about the whole story. "And what were you doing on the beach at that hour, Willow?" *Oh, joy. I sound just like Mom.* But she continued doggedly, "I mean, predawn walks on the beach might be romantic to some, but—"

Oz, shaking his head, murmured, "Couldn't. Full moon."

Buffy stared at Willow, waiting for an answer.

"I didn't have a choice," the redhead explained indignantly. "I'm an E.L.F.!"

There was a rather startled pause in the room. The selkie girl looked curiously at each of the others in the room, distracted from her own misery by the sudden change in everyone's posture.

"O . . . kay," Buffy said slowly, then turned to her Watcher. "I don't have to stake elves, do I?"

He frowned, equally confused. "Well, no, I don't believe—"

"An E.L.F.," Willow repeated in exasperation. "E, period, L, period, F, period. Emergency Local Force. My dad got me into it, part of his Wildlife Rescue membership. I've been doing it for years. Well, not *doing* it, 'cause we haven't had to, but ready, anyway." Blank looks of incomprehension greeted her.

"We're volunteers. When there's something like this, like the oil spill, they call us. Because we're local. And so we were there. On the beach. Where I found her." Willow stopped short, frowning. "Look, I've been up since, like, three A.M., and I'm starting to get cranky, and we need to figure out what we're going to do!"

Buffy glanced at the selkie, who looked back at her with rounded eyes like a puppy. *Yeah, right, a seal pup, that is.* "First, we've got to figure out how long it's going to take to dry-clean the coat. Right? And then find her a place to stay."

Xander snorted. "And where's that going to be? I mean, your mom can be kinda clueless sometimes,

Will, but even she's going to notice someone sleeping in the tub. Especially one filled with water."

"Forget about my house," Buffy said. "My mom's got enough weirdness to deal with already. And Xander and Oz are out too, I'd guess."

Xander nodded emphatically. Oz considered it, momentarily, then shook his head. "Would cause problems," was all he said.

"I will take her in."

When everyone looked at the Watcher, he shrugged, gesturing faintly with the hand which held his glasses. "I have the room, certainly. And if anyone asks, we will merely say that she is . . . ah, the daughter of a friend."

Xander shrugged. "And she's young enough nobody's gonna think anything's, y'know, kinky. Not that they would."

"Thank you, Xander. I think."

Ignoring the usual bickering behind her, Buffy knelt by the chair where the selkie huddled.

"Hi, there."

There was no response, only the solemn, brown-eyed stare that was starting to wig Buffy out a little. *Do selkies blink?* she wondered.

"Not much on the talking, huh?" Oz asked, coming over as well.

"You two should really be able to bond," Buffy told him, getting to her feet and backing away. *Okay, so harmless. I mean, how much damage can a little seal-girl do, right? They eat fish, not people.*

"That's us, the small, silent types," Oz said.

"She didn't make a sound the whole time we were coming over here." Willow, thankful that the problem was now a shared one, sounded a little calmer now.

"Not even when I tried to get her on my bicycle, to get her here. You think maybe she can't talk?"

"Like the Little Mermaid," Buffy agreed, "trading her voice for legs."

"Seals are normally quite vocal," Giles commented, "so I would suppose that it's more a matter of her not knowing human speech. A stranger in a strange land. So to speak."

Absently replacing his glasses, he went to a shelf of oversized hardcover books and began browsing. "Fortunately, selkies are rather popular in modern mythology, so there's a great deal written about them. Unfortunately—"

"The trick's going to be figuring out what's true from all the legend stuff, huh?" Willow exchanged a knowing glance with the Watcher, then sighed. "Oh well. Better too much information than none at all."

"It's a nice change," Xander agreed. "But not nice if you're going to make us read all of it," he added quickly. "I hereby designate myself Go-For-Donuts Boy."

The clock ticked over to 7:45, and the bell rang through the library, causing the selkie girl to start out of the chair like a spooked rabbit.

"Whoa, Ariel," Oz said soothingly, putting up a hand that stopped just shy of actually touching her. "Easy now."

"Ariel?" Buffy asked.

He shrugged, looking a little embarrassed. "Yeah. Like you said, the Little Mermaid. Not having a voice."

Willow beamed. "Yeah. It's perfect."

"Perfect," Giles cut in, "would be no one being late to class this early in the term. You *do* have classes now . . . ?"

17

"French!" Buffy wailed.

Willow's eyes widened in horror. "Oh, Calculus! Uh, Giles, you'll be all right?"

The Watcher already had his head in a book. Waving absently at them all, he said, "Don't worry. I have a great deal of experience playing . . . babysitter."

The phenomenon of a selkie in the library wasn't enough to keep the more mundane details of high school from taking their toll. Students went to class, sat in class, got up, made it to another class, maybe found time to hit the bathroom in between. Buffy managed to lose herself in the boring pattern. When she wasn't out saving the world, it was an almost refreshingly mind-numbing way to pass a couple of hours.

"Yeah, I think I really almost aced the test," Buffy began as she and Xander escaped their shared horror of World History and headed determinedly down the hallway, intent on finding Will and Oz and collapsing for lunch. "But I—"

"Well, if it isn't the Loser Patrol," a too-familiar voice said brightly.

Buffy winced. Cordelia. *I really, really don't need this today,* Buffy thought. *Or, in fact, any day.* She quickly stepped between Xander and his ex-girlfriend.

Not quickly enough.

"Oh look, it's Miss Congeniality," Xander responded. "Where's the rest of your little clique? Still parking their brooms?"

"Xander, down boy," Buffy ordered.

"That's nice, Buffy," Cordy purred. "Do you have him trained to the leash, too?"

Without waiting for a response, she turned and headed away from them, her heels clicking sharply against the floor. Everyone in the hallway stepped aside to clear a path for her. Social pariah or not, you didn't want to cross Cordelia Chase when she was in that kind of mood or ever.

Xander let out his breath in a gusty sigh. "She's such a—"

"No," Buffy said flatly. "Stop it. Enough already, okay? If you can't be civil, then just don't talk to each other. Honestly, I think I liked the two of you better when you were smooching in the broom closet every other minute."

"Hey, it's not like I started it—" Xander protested.

"No, but you can finish it, okay?"

Xander shrugged in a Yeah, Sure, Whatever way. Buffy shook her head. Although she would never admit it, she missed having Cordelia around. The entire relationship polka her friends had gone through had really messed up Slayerette logistics, and things had been rocky for a while among her buds.

But things seemed to be okay between Will and Xander and Oz now, so she wasn't going to rock the boat. Cordy would come around. Or not.

Everyone was staring at her. They'd seen her talking to her ex-loser boyfriend and Buffy, and now they were staring. Staring, and not talking, and . . . *Okay,* Cordelia told herself. *Moving on, Chase. Keep moving. If you stop now, someone will say something. If they say anything, you'll have to acknowledge them, so keep moving . . .*

No good. She needed to get out of sight, at least for a minute. Her hand tightened, and she was reminded of the book she carried. Library. Right. Extremely over-due book, which would mean extremely pissy librarian. What is it with them, anyway? It's not like anyone else was going to take books out or anything. Nobody was ever in the library except Buffy and her losers, and they'd all be in lunch, so all she'd have to deal with would be—

"Hey, Giles? I was just coming by to return that book you loaned me. The one with the really gross goat-creature thing? Definitely weird—Oh. Hey there."

The girl curled up in the library chair couldn't have been more than . . . oh, maybe ten? Eleven? Definitely young. That sleek cap of brown hair could have used a trim, but it kind of fit the triangular face. And the girl had the biggest brown eyes Cordelia had ever seen, al-most completely round, like a penny.

Giles wasn't in the vicinity.

Cordy walked over to the girl.

"So who're you, huh? Did you land on Giles' doorstep this morning, or what?"

The kid tilted her head up at that, chin first, but didn't say a thing. Foreign, Cordelia guessed. Not French, she would have heard about a new French fam-ily moving in. Maybe Russian? She had that look. A refugee from somewhere, that was certain. *Oh great, now we're taking in strays.* Those were definitely someone else's clothes she was wearing, not at all be-coming.

"This isn't a good place to hang, you know," Cordelia said, pleased to pass this tidbit along. "Not a single magazine under six months old, and the pictures in his books you should definitely not be looking at. Give you nightmares for a month. And I bet he hasn't even thought you might not be comfortable in that big chair, has he?"

At that moment, Giles came out of his office, a book under one arm, another open in his hands, and his attention solidly on the page he was reading. "What? Oh, yes, hello, Cordelia."

"New assistant? Or new demon?" Cordelia gestured to the girl in the chair.

"Ah no, I'm, um, watching her for the morning. Yes, thank you for returning the book, I assume without coffee stains this time?"

His tone was brusque, his attention clearly still on the material in his hands.

"As pristine as ever," she said coolly. "And completely useless. Remind me next time to try a source that's not a century out of date."

"Yes, fine."

"Fine."

Cordelia dropped the book down on the counter, and made as dramatic an exit as she could manage with an audience of none.

CHAPTER 3

"A selkie?"

"That's what Giles says." Buffy paused, whirled, and staked a stocky male vampire who had just come running at them, and shook her head. "Is it just me, or are the vamps in this town starting to show a serious lack of anything resembling style? I mean, my *mom* could have taken him out."

She brushed herself off, frowning at the mess on her black long-sleeved top. "Got to remember to wear something that doesn't show the dust so much."

"So we've got selkies in town now?" Angel prodded her as they resumed walking through the moonlit graveyard. The night after the full moon, so Xander was on wolf-watch duty while Willow and Giles waded through the research, trying to find something that would help them deal with Giles's little house-guest.

"Oh. Yeah. Selkie, of the singular. Is that the singular? Or is it like sheep?"

"Selkie for both, I think." He shrugged, moving around a slightly tilting headstone and stepping carefully over a gaping hole in the turf where a grave used to be. "I was never much on that particular legend, though. It always seemed a children's story, a way for some families to claim something special about themselves, and not very interesting." He looked sideways at her. "Buffy, what's wrong?"

She shrugged. "Nothing."

"Nothing," Angel repeated flatly. "You've been tense all night. And don't tell me it's work-related. Town's been quiet all week, but not so quiet you should be jumpy. And it can't be the selkie. You're more than capable of handling one little, perfectly normal addition to the town's population." He caught himself. "Well, normal for Sunnydale, anyhow."

Buffy cracked just the slightest smile at that. "Job gets to me sometimes, that's all."

"You want to talk about it?"

"Not really, no. Besides, we've got company."

Buffy caught a female vamp by the arm, swung her at Angel for him to dispatch, then kicked a male vamp in the knee. As he crumpled, she ducked up under the grasping arms of a third vamp, said, "Nighty-night," and staked him. The vamp she'd knee-hauled rushed her from behind, but Buffy ducked and sent him flying over her head. He twisted as he landed, tried leaping back up at her—and ran right onto the stake.

"Buh-*bye!*" Buffy said in her best flight attendant voice.

"Feel better?" Angel asked.

"Actually . . . yes." She perked up, flashing him an unforced grin. "Sometimes it's good to be me."

"So what is it that's bothering you?"

"Angel . . ." Buffy stopped, her good mood fleeing as quickly as it had arrived. But she could tell from the look in his eyes that he wasn't going to be put off. *Never fails. When it comes to our un-relationship, he dances around the facts like Fred Astaire,* she thought. *But when it comes to stuff that doesn't deal with Us, he's like . . . like something really irritating.*

Angel waited, patient. She would tell him. She always did.

"Nothing. I'm of the calm. Completely. It's just . . . what *do* you know about selkies?"

Angel frowned slightly, clearly casting his memory back to his distant childhood, remembering what he could. "Basic Celtic legend, popular along the coastal towns. Fishermen told the stories, mostly. They're seals in the sea, human-looking on the land, need magical sealskins to shapeshift—but I take it you already know that."

"Difficult to miss," Buffy said dryly. "What with the selkie currently minus a working skin and shacking up at Giles's place, and all."

"Almost all the legends I can recall deal with adults, a few male selkies trying to attract human women, but mostly females who're captured by human males and taken as wives. Sometimes happily, more often not. Like I said, lots of families try to use the legend to pump up their own history. There are supposed to be some of their selkie/human great-great-grandchildren running around today, webbed fingers and toes all that's left of their selkie blood."

Buffy glanced automatically at her hands, caught Angel watching her, and said quickly, "So there's no way they can be evil, right?"

The vampire frowned, thinking it over. "Well . . . no. Not evil. Cruel, sometimes, by human standards, I suppose. But Giles would know more about that sort of thing than I would."

At that moment, a vamp leaped out from behind a stone monument, hesitating when it saw who was there.

"Mr. Lawrence. I was wondering when you'd come back to make my life miserable again." Buffy sighed and went forward to meet her former Driver's Ed instructor, stake in hand.

"Actually," Giles admitted somewhat reluctantly, glancing up from the latest in the growing pile of books on his desk, "I don't know very much about selkies at all. As they're generally considered, well, rather benign, there wasn't much reason to learn about them."

"Or to do any real research about them, apparently," Willow said in disgust, closing another book and adding it to her pile of discards by the sofa. They had moved their base of operations to Giles's apartment for the duration, in order to keep Ariel as out of sight as possible. The addition of the books from the library to the books Giles already had made his apartment look like an explosion in a binding factory. But neither human nor the selkie appeared to notice, stepping over the piles and shifting tomes as needed, without conscious thought.

"How can so many books be so completely useless? And the websites—" Willow snorted in disdain. "A lot of fluff and fairy tales that don't even match up with what's in the older legends, like people just made it all up."

"They probably did," Giles reminded her. "If you don't believe something is real, what's to stop you from adding your own interpretation? It's the curse of the serious folklorist or, for that matter, occultist."

Ariel, still wearing Willow's castoffs, was curled at the other end of the sofa, watching the two humans. She still held onto the sealskin, but her eyes were less wary, her body language a little more relaxed. Getting her into Giles's car had taken some doing—prompting Xander to comment that even selkies knew the vehicle was a deathtrap—but once inside the dark, cool air of the apartment, the selkie had settled down to the point where even sudden loud noises like the phone ringing didn't startle her too badly.

"Yes . . ." Giles continued, flipping open another text and scanning it quickly before setting it aside. Looking up at Willow, he continued, "The more romantic legends do seem to appeal to a certain element of the population. And, as I said, selkies tend not to be the sort of creature with whom past Watchers have concerned themselves."

He leaned back in the chair, reaching for his cup of tea and taking a sip. "As a race, they tend to be standoffish, except of course in those rare cases when one comes to shore to take a human mate. Although," he added, "very few of those cases have ever been substantiated by anything other than family legend. It's really rather inconvenient."

Willow snorted again, a distinctly indelicate sound. "I'll say! For everything that's been written in all these books, it's all the same information over and over again. And half of it contradicts the other, and, and . . ."

"Welcome to the wonderful world of secondary source research. Now you know why I prefer to use primary sources." Giles frowned suddenly. "Of course, why didn't I—" Pushing away from his desk, he tapped his hand against the pile of books, thinking, then snapped his fingers and headed for the stairs that led to the upper level of the apartment.

"Giles?" Willow called after him.

Ariel looked up, her brown gaze tracking between Willow and the stairs as though asking where the big male had gone.

"Hey, it's okay," Willow soothed. " 'S'okay."

Reassured, the selkie settled back into the blanket, making a soft moaning noise that the best website on harbor seals Willow had found had described as indicating satisfaction. Well, for seals, anyway. It might mean something really different for selkies. Or not. She wasn't sure how much of that stuff applied to selkies. Some stuff about wolves carried over to werewolves, though; they knew that for a fact. So it was a place to start, anyway.

Following the advice the website had given, Willow extended her hand, palm down, and rested it on the sofa cushion an unthreatening distance from her companion. The more she did it, the faster Ariel would come to accept it as comforting. Supposedly.

"If we're going to help you," she said conversationally, "we're really going to have to take a closer look at that skin. And you. Which means you're going to have to trust us. 'Cause otherwise, you're kinda stuck here. And here's really not a good place for you to be, if you know what I mean." Willow rolled her eyes at her own words. "Which you don't. On account of the not speaking English thing. That's a problem we haven't had before."

The thought struck her. "Wow. That's right. All the demons speak English. Is it, like, the official language of Hell, or do they have some kind of demonic universal translator? A spell like that could be really useful for French class—Hey, Giles! Find anything?"

He came down the stairs, pausing on the bottom step, to glance at the book in his hand. "As a matter of fact, yes, I believe I have. Honigsberg and O'Hogan's *Treoir Praiticuil Muiri.*"

Ariel straightened with a startled little whine rising from deep in her throat. Giles, still looking only at the book, continued, "That's Irish Gaelic; the English would be *Practical Marine Guide.* I picked it up at a small bookstore a few years ago, along with several other titles; never had a chance to do more than browse through it—"

"Giles, no, wait! You said the title, in Gaelic, I mean, and she—Ariel, do you speak Gaelic? I don't, but— Giles?"

Giles looked from Willow to the selkie, noting the look of interest in the creature's large brown eyes. "Actually, I don't speak it very well myself . . . um . . . *Caintigh Gaelige?*"

Ariel made a noise that, coming from a normal human kid, would have been a giggle. *"Se'fo'd'ach."*

"Hey!" Willow cried. "She spoke!"

Giles blinked. "I *think* she just called me . . . silly." His expression said that he wasn't sure if he should be insulted or not. "Her accent certainly isn't any better than mine, and I admit that my command of the syntax is rusty, but . . ."

He tried a few more phrases, stumbling over the grammar. But Ariel, though she listened with great interest, didn't volunteer anything else.

Giles finally gave up with a sigh. "At a guess, her people know Gaelic only as a second language, some remnant perhaps from a time when they were more closely affiliated with fishermen and such along the coastline of their home islands. But the differences between the words and pronunciation I know, and what she seems to speak, do not give one much hope for communication."

He brandished the *Treoir Praiticuil Muiri*. "But at least, we know we are on the correct track."

The book didn't look very impressive, Willow thought. Unlike a lot of Giles's other books, it was bound in ordinary paper and cardboard, like something one would see in any run-of-the-mill bookstore. She held out her hand, and he gave it to her readily—okay, so it was written in a language she couldn't read. That was a point in its favor. Very little of the really interesting stuff was written in modern English.

"Anything else useful there?" she asked, handing it back to Giles.

"Perhaps . . . See, here . . . wait . . . something about 'by the wave's side, by the wave's side, um . . . *go brach* . . .' "

"Go brach," Ariel echoed eagerly, as though prompting him. *"Go deo!"* Her voice was soft, but deeper than a human girl's of that age would be.

"Forever!" Giles finished in triumph. " 'By the wave's side forever'—it's a charm for a changeling, perhaps a descendant of a selkie and a human who wished to go to sea."

"But that isn't going to get the skin clean."

"Er, no." Giles leafed busily through the book. "I really do need to brush up on my Gaelic."

"Maybe I could find something on the Internet, with alternate pronunciations?" Willow suggested hopefully.

Giles shrugged. "It is certainly worth a look. Although I can't imagine anyone putting together such an arcane bit of information."

Willow made a face at him. "Believe me, if it's weird, or a waste of time, it's on the Internet."

"Which rather proves my point about the whole thing, doesn't it?" It was a long-running argument, and one they both knew wasn't going to be resolved any time soon.

"There do seem to be some rather intriguing paragraphs about the original selkies' homes and their migratory patterns," Giles began, returning to the original topic of conversation—

"Rachaidh me ann go!" Ariel burst out, and looked hopefully at them both.

" 'I will go back again,' " Giles translated after a hesitant moment. "I think."

"She wants to go home," Willow echoed. "Poor thing."

"Quite the change from our usual brand of crisis," Giles agreed, settling himself down to study the book further. "A welcome change, indeed."

The late-day sun cast long shadows on the now-deserted beach. The truck and rescue workers were long gone for the day, and the quiet sea was empty of containment ships. An occasional splotch of black scum still coated the sand and rocks, and come morning, more volunteers would come to take samples of the water and sand, but for the most part, the cleanup—both that of humans and Mother Nature—was finished here. The work had all moved indoors, to the facility in San Diego, where lab techs, doctors, and volunteers were working on the animals which had been brought in from all along the coastline. In a few days, the surviving rescued animals, healthy again, would be returned to their native habitat.

The only living thing to be seen on this stretch of beach was a man, hands in the pockets of his dark brown windbreaker. He stood on the shoulder of the road, his rental car parked a few feet behind him.

Too late. Again.

He stepped over the low cement wall and walked down the sand to the water's edge. Standing there, the sun slanting directly into his grim, sharply-angled face and glinting off his straight, graying black hair, he stared out over the waves, searching for something just below the surface.

"Where are you?" he asked the emptiness. "Where are you?" The words were soft, but the voice was angry.

There was no reply, except the single caw of a gull that whirled overhead once before winging farther out to sea and disappearing into the sunset.

The man looked up at the bird, identifying and dismissing it with a single quick thought before returning to his study of the water. Then with a shrug he walked down the beach, his gaze now focused on the sand, smoothed by the tide from the turmoil of that morning. Now and again, something would catch his attention, and he would bend to examine it. Or he would move into the occasional grouping of rocks, running his hands over the cool surfaces of the outcroppings.

His entire posture was that of a man on a mission. Of a man determined to find something . . . whether it was there or not.

Then a shrill *brrring* cut into the silence, and he straightened, pulling out a small cell phone.

"Dr. Lee here," he barked into it. "What have you got for me?"

The answer clearly didn't please him.

"Idiots! If you had gotten word to me sooner—" He reined in his temper with an effort, listening to the hasty excuses of his staff. "Fine. I want the names of all the rescue workers, everyone who had anything to do with the cleanup."

He took a look around again, frowning. It had become too dark to continue his search.

"No. The report from Los Angeles was quite clear on that. At least one of them was caught in the spill, which means it will be helpless until it can rejoin its herd. I don't intend for it to get away.

"Not this time."

He closed the phone and put it away, then stared off into the horizon, where the blue-gray of the water met the gray-blue of the sky and merged.

"Not again."

CHAPTER 4

"**O**kay, that's it. I mean, absolutely, it. Next time, Giles gets cleanup duty."

Joyce looked up in surprise as her daughter came storming through the front door. Her hair was plastered to her head, and a strange bluish goo coated her arms and torso.

"Oh dear." Joyce struggled not to laugh. She supposed that she should be concerned, but the fact that Buffy was clearly unharmed . . . The laughter burst free. "Oh dear. Oh, oh dear."

"Thanks, Mom."

Joyce fought herself back to calmness. "Dare I ask what all . . . that, is?"

"Goon."

"Goon?"

"Goon," Buffy confirmed. "Big, blue, ugly."

"Exploding?"

"Exploding. Giles tells me to stake it, so I stake it, and—" she made a gesture to indicate her slimed state.

Joyce took one look at her daughter's disgruntled expression and burst into laughter again.

"Mom!" Buffy said indignantly.

"Go on upstairs, wash that stuff off you. A long hot bath, and you'll feel better."

Buffy shuddered, a long, drawn-out quake that stopped Joyce's laughter dead. "Think I'll pass on the bath, actually. Hey, it's okay, honest. Just tired, that's all. Long patrol. Night, Mom."

"Night, sweetie," Joyce said, and fought back a sigh. Some people had daughters who were obsessed with boys, or rock music, or weird cults. She had a daughter who came home at 1 A.M. covered with exploded blue goon.

Shaking her head, Joyce went back to the late movie on TV.

Dr. Lee stared at the display on his computer screen, one finger tapping against his lips. The swirls of blue and green and black tangled in endless swirls and circles, a display of technological mastery over the earth's currents.

Or at least the illusion of mastery, he thought dourly.

He pushed away from his desk with a sigh. The land masses of the planet were mapped and regulated, spotted from orbit and lined with human footprints. The secrets it held were merely undiscovered for now, the hidden knowledge within human reach.

But over three-fourths of the earth was covered with water. Now there, *there* were secrets worthy of discovery. The ocean flowed endlessly, utterly unconcerned with what occurred on the planet's land masses. It was an alien world, full of sharp noises and dark silences, and for all humanity's vaunted claims, it was still untamed, still relatively unplundered.

It was merciless, and cruel, to those who did not belong to its depths.

Lee reached out to turn off the display, then paused, his fingers resting on the screen.

"So cruel," he repeated softly.

Something stirred, far below the surface of the deep waters off the California coast, under the patterns of the never-resting currents. Something that stretched long arms and legs, then flexed clawed hands and sped upward, heading unerringly toward some distant goal. It broke the surface, gasping as its lungs switched to breathing air, then glanced quickly about. In the dim light of moon on water, it looked . . . almost human.

Then the creature saw a quick splash as a fish broke the surface. The being lunged forward, and clawed hands closed on the fish. It bit down—

Then spat in disgust. Poisoned! Inedible—tainted with the foulness which had ruined their other feeding places as well.

Enough, it thought bitterly. *Too much. For too long.*

The creature dove again, forcing out the air, gills taking in the blessedly clean water below.

"*Come,*" the being called in the silent language of the sea, too high-pitched for human ears to follow. "*Attend.*"

Others swam up to it, their shapes, like its own, vaguely human. But no human ever had hair like flowing green seaweed. No human ever had faintly scaled gray-green skin.

And no human ever bore a mouth filled with sharp, shark-like fangs.

"Brothers," the first one called to its kin. *"There is new prey to be had."*

"Shipwreck?" another asked hungrily. *"Bodies floating, salt and sweet?"*

"There are no ships," a third snapped, fangs biting down on empty air in frustration. *"This is a poor hunting domain! We have tasted fish, only fish, for far too long—and now even the fish are tainted! This is no way for hunters to live!"*

The others in the pack nodded agreement. Merrows, the dark kin to mermaids, fed mostly on flesh and blood—fish and seal, mainly, human flesh and blood when they could get it. Ever since humanity had sailed the seas, merrows had harrowed their ships, causing wrecks, and dragging unwary sailors overboard to feed on them.

But ships were made of metals now, and were harder to capsize. Men listened with machines, not their ears, and were more difficult to lure. None in this school had ever tasted human flesh.

"We live as I say it!" the first merrow spat. *"Unless you would challenge for the leadership?"*

There was an uneasy moment of first and third merrow circling each other . . . then the third merrow backed off, hanging submissively limp in the water. The first merrow gave what might have been a smile or a snarl. *"There is an easier way to hunt. A more pleasant way to hunt."*

They were listening now, avid.

"*Haven't you seen them there at the shore, almost in the waves? Daring to enter our domain on their wave-gliders, their small craft that could not stop a pup—playing in the surf as though we did not exist!*"

The other merrows stirred uneasily. "*What? What? Hunt near land? Hunt on land?*"

"*Just that,*" the first merrow told them, and waited till the anxious swirlings about had stopped.

"*We have never hunted on land!*" came a protest.

"*Till now,*" the first countered.

"*That is not our way! We are slow, clumsy, out of water, on dry land!*"

"*They come to our waters, survive there. They adapt. So too will we. Quick attacks, out and back again.*"

The merrow paused to lick sharp teeth with a tongue that was vaguely serpentine. "*They have forgotten us, the humans. They are not wary. We shall see that they remember.*"

He stopped, sinking up to his eyes below the water's surface in a classic pre-attack pose.

"*We shall see that they do not foul our hunting grounds again.*"

"Ah?"

Giles winced. Ariel's voice could take on a piercing quality when she was curious about something. "Lamp," he explained, "er . . . *lampa,* not that your people would know anything about—no, that's—"

"Ah?"

"A paperweight," Giles finished, snatching it from her hands before the selkie could drop it. "And no, I haven't a clue as to the proper Gaelic word."

"Ah?"

"Chair. That's right. To sit in. Like the other chairs you've asked me about."

He stopped. Ariel, now perched on the chair in question, was looking up at him with her huge eyes, innocence and confusion there. *A child,* he reminded himself. *Not human, but just a child.*

One who was already starting to look exhausted ... no, rather, dried out. A selkie could stay out of the sea indefinitely, if the folklore was correct, but there were limits.

Bathtub, Giles thought. Water salted, of course, to make it properly briny. A good long soak should help her.

And, hopefully, he added to himself, snatching the paperweight from her hand again just in time, *tire her out as well!*

"Buffy ..."

Buffy turned on her side, snuggling deeper into the sheets. Nice dream. Much better than the usual. She could almost feel Angel's presence with her, holding her, his hands cool and smooth ...

"Buffy!"

His voice sounding really, really worried. Rolling onto her back, Buffy opened her eyes.

Angel was perched outside the window, tapping lightly on it to wake her.

"Oh, sorry," she said, and got out of bed to unlock the window sash and let him in. Her mother must have gone on another crime prevention jag—like there were just so many burglars wandering around Sunnydale after dark!

The sky outside was nearing false dawn, and as the vampire climbed in through the open window, she looked at him in surprise, wondering what could have brought him out this late.

"We've got a problem," he told her. "Maybe a big one. Willy passed along a rumor, more reliable than most of his, so I dropped in on a few folks, checked it out."

"Y'know, some guys bring flowers, candy . . ." She sighed, giving up. "Okay. What rumor? Details first, then panic."

Angel nodded, sitting on the edge of her bed. "Some of the local vampires heard that there were a lot of people down by the beach a couple of towns over early yesterday morning."

"The rescue team," Buffy said. "There was an oil spill. The cleanup's still going on, I guess, the wildlife do-gooders were down there—" She broke off in sudden alarm. "I told Willow it was dangerous for her to be out there alone! All right, never mind that. How many did the vamps get?"

"None."

Buffy stopped in the process of reaching for her clothes. "None? Then what's the—"

"The vampires decided to check it out, looking for a snack before turning in for the day, and there were already dead bodies on the beach. Humans, four of them. Some kids who'd gone down that night to have a bonfire, or something, I guess. Or maybe some of those 'do-gooders' not knowing when to quit. They do now," he added.

"Already dead?" Buffy repeated.

"Their throats were torn open, the bodies left lying on the sand."

"Not vampires?"

"I don't think so. We're not real big on salt water. Any water, actually. You never know who's been praying over it."

Buffy looked at him suspiciously. "That was a joke?"

"Mostly." He tried to smile, then shook his head. "Buffy, this wasn't a vampire attack. That much, everyone's agreed. Blood was spilled everywhere, like a wild animal attack. But that doesn't make sense either. What kind of animal would attack and then not eat their kill?"

"Okay, thank you very much for that visual. So, what?"

"They don't know. But the vampires I talked to—"

Buffy snorted, knowing Angel's usual means of interrogation for his fellow demons.

"They're nervous, Buffy. Whatever it is, they don't like it. They said they could feel it watching them from the water, like something huge and malevolent. And these are not demons with well-developed imaginations."

Buffy sat down on the bed next to him, staring into emptiness.

"Buffy?"

"Water," she murmured. "Water, and death. Darn it, I *told* Giles that dream was prophetic!"

As soon as Angel was gone to a safer daytime hideyhole, Buffy hit the phone, dialing the number from memory. A groggy voice answered, "Yes . . . ?"

"Giles. Me. Buffy."

"Buffy, I—" His voice moved away from the earpiece for a moment, and, dimly, she heard him speaking, ". . . Ariel, no! . . . into *everything*. Like babysitting a ferret . . ."

But then his sleepy voice sharpened, returning to her. "What's wrong?"

"We've got to meet, Giles. Soonest. And we're going to need major old book stuff."

Hellmouth-trained reactions: He didn't waste time asking questions. "The library," Giles said, "one hour," and hung up.

CHAPTER 5

It might be Saturday, Buffy thought, but the high school custodial crew had long become accustomed to the sight and sounds of people in the library over the weekend. They did their cleanup quickly, at odd hours, and steered clear of that part of the building the rest of the time.

After hanging up the phone with Giles, Buffy had called Willow, who in turn had contacted Oz and Xander, letting them know the sitch.

One of these days, Buffy thought, *we're all going to have to get beepers. Or walkie-talkies. Or something. Because leaving a message, "Yes, Mrs. Rosenberg, we've got dead bodies, and I need Willow to help save the world again," is so not possible.*

Once everyone had arrived, Buffy broke the news. "All right. New crisis of the day. We've got four bodies on the beach, throats torn out, pieces, uh, missing—and

Angel says the local undead community doesn't have a happy on about it."

"Oh, great," Xander said, slumping even farther down in his chair, his legs stretched out in front of him. "Something that chews on humans and makes vampires nervous. Why am I thinking *not* a good monster to have in town?"

"Well, excuse me," Buffy retorted, forcing herself to stand in one place when what she really wanted to do was pace. "I'm sorry if I'm bringing news that inconveniences anyone." Okay, so she was grumpy. Deal. She didn't like unknown threats. Especially ones that woke her up from nice dreams.

Giles frowned from where he sat on the library steps. "But we don't actually know that it wasn't a vampire attack?"

He was looking a little less than his usual Watcherly self. Unwilling to leave Ariel alone in his apartment, he had carted her along with him. Dressed in pale gray sweatpants and a cute pink top that screamed "Willow's closet," she had taken one look at the grim faces of the humans around her, and promptly curled up against the Englishman like a limpet, mumbling into the tweed of his jacket. He had finally given up trying to unattach her, so there he sat, holding her in a comforting hug.

"Cute," Willow had whispered to Buffy, when they'd first seen that. Buffy had only nodded, her attention on the news she was bringing.

Now, she studied the selkie more carefully. It should have given Buffy a warm happy glowy feeling, seeing her Watcher turned to complete mush by 75 pounds of brown-eyed kidlet, but every time she looked at them, a weird, cold feeling tried to sneak into her brain. Selkie. Water creature. Attacks on a beach.

Okay, so it was a reach, hooking a little kid with that kind of vicious attack. But maybe adults, grown-up selkies, looking for her? Maybe the kids spooked them or got in the way, and—

No, if she was going to be honest, that sour feeling in her gut when she looked at Ariel wasn't a Slayer thing—at least, she didn't think so. It felt . . . way too much like . . . something else. Like jealousy. Which would be a bad. So she looked away, and focused herself on the problem at hand.

"Angel says he's sure. Definitely not vampires."

"Well, he would know," Willow agreed.

Oz, being Oz, cut directly to the point. "And Ariel? Since the beach is where Will found her."

Buffy shot a quick look at Oz. "I was wondering that," she said, trying not to see how Giles's expression got that closed-in look, like it did whenever she said something he didn't approve of.

"She couldn't have anything to do with that!" Willow protested immediately, rising to the defense of her foundling.

"Yes, I must agree with Willow," Giles said. "Ignoring the fact that she was in my apartment all last night, sleeping quite soundly—after dismantling most of the furnishings," he added wryly, "I cannot think of a single instance wherein a selkie has shown violent tendencies, much less the ability to attack and kill a human. The worst thing ever said of them was that they were prone to cutting fishermen's nets to free their kin."

"So it couldn't maybe be her folks, come looking to take her home?" Buffy asked.

"It would seem unlikely. The fact that she was on the beach, alone, in such conditions, would suggest that, ah . . ." Giles stumbled over the rest of the sentence, as Ariel looked up at him with an inquiring whine.

"That her folks aren't in any position to come for her?" Willow finished for him.

"Yes."

"Okay, so scratch that possibility," Buffy said, taking charge once again. "But Oz is right, there's way too much coincidence here." And now she did begin pacing, trying to get some of that nervous energy pumped up into her brain. "So we've got a selkie caught in an oil slick, and her coat all damaged because of it. Which, if you're right, means she can't put it on and shift, which means she can't go back home."

Giles nodded. "Without the ability to change her shape, Ariel is quite defenseless, even more so than a normal human child her age, since she is not accustomed to being on land for extended periods of time."

"And we've got the same beach, not even twenty-four hours later, and four dead people as decoration. Throats cut, nastily gory, with just enough body parts missing to suggest someone had a beach-side breakfast party."

"Kind of like a shark," Xander mused. *"Jaws,* only not in water." He deepened his voice, quoting, "This was no boating accident."

"Could've been sharks," Oz said. "Seeing as how it happened outside Sunnydale."

"Do we know for a fact that the victims weren't swimming?" Giles asked Buffy.

"Were, maybe, before the being killed part. But they

were found up on the beach, not in the surf, and sharks aren't normally known for getting out of the water."

"They do get people in the shallows, sometimes," Willow said helpfully. "But then they usually drag their prey down farther into the water, and all in little bits and chum and stuff," she added. "And I think I watch too much *Animal Planet*."

"Besides," Buffy countered, "I don't think the vamps would have gotten so uptight about a shark staring at them. Your basic Great White isn't exactly going to be cutting in on their turf."

"So . . . something else. Something that maybe got tangled in the oil slick, too?" Oz asked.

"Or," Giles said thoughtfully, "perhaps had their normal food source damaged by the oil . . ."

He struggled to his feet, hampered by Ariel, who was still hanging on tightly. "Ariel, child, do let go. You're safe . . . uh . . . *sabhailte*. That's right. Safe. Let go."

As the selkie sat, dejected, on the stairs, Giles hunted through the library stacks. Willow called to him, "Sea beings, right?"

"Water-based, yes. If we are to assume the vampires were correct in the threat coming from the ocean. Preferably local, but don't overlook anything because of geographic limitations—the sea encourages migration by its current patterns."

"Okay." She turned on the library computer, dialed into the Internet, and begin searching the web. "Ocean, mythology, unexplained deaths, shark attacks . . . anyone got another keyword?"

"Mutilations?" Xander suggested.

"Mutilations. Good."

Oz pushed his chair back and went into Giles's office to plug in the coffeemaker. It sounded like it was going to be a long day, and he was coming off three very unrestful nights.

"Willow? You want some tea?"

Willow nodded absently, already engrossed in the material loading onto her screen. "Uh-huh. Ginger Twist, please? Lots of sugar."

Buffy and Xander exchanged resigned glances. "Here," Buffy said, handing him a heavy book labeled *World Folklore,* and picked *World Mythology* off the shelf for herself. "They also serve who sit and read."

Oz came out after a few minutes, cup of coffee in one hand, mug of tea in the other. He put the mug next to Willow, a careful distance away from the computer but still within reach, and sat down next to her with his coffee, picking out a couple of books for himself. Silence fell after that, the only noises the clicking of Willow's keyboard, the occasional sips of hot liquids, and the soft crackle of pages turning. Even Giles's movements on the level above them seemed subdued, the sound of his shoes on the flooring quieter than usual.

Then Xander broke the silence, triumphantly exclaiming, "Serras!"

"I'm afraid that those are monsters of the deep sea," Giles told him, coming down the stairs, more books in his arms. "They have never been recorded as entering shallow water."

"A karad?" Buffy suggested, finger marking her place on the page. "It's even local. There're stories about it from way back before anyone but the Indians were here."

"Let me see," Willow said, scooting over to take a look at what Buffy was reading. "Supposed to eat sailors, hunts at night, yeah, may—oh. No."

Buffy frowned. "What? Why not?"

"Look. No teeth. It's supposed to swallow 'em whole."

"Oh. Right."

"Danavas . . ." Giles murmured. "Demon of the sea . . . no, that's strictly India . . . a bit too far . . . and he isn't listed as a flesh eater."

"What about Paikea?" Willow suggested, going back to her computer screen. "I mean, he's supposed to be some sort of Hawaiian sea-monster god—No, forget it. Says he's way territorial, wouldn't leave the area. Besides, he doesn't go in for human-eating. Which makes him a *good* sea monster."

"Leaving Hawaii for Sunnydale. Nope, can't see it," Oz said, then coughed a little as dust rose from the book he had cracked open.

"Giles?" Buffy called up to him. "This isn't going to work, is it? I mean, just about everyone with a beach seems to have come up with a sea monster or something."

"Precisely the problem." Giles gave Ariel an absent-minded pat on the head as he passed her, then sat at a table, brow furrowed. "Right," he said after a moment, tapping the top of the table with one hand, thinking. "Buffy, I want you to check out the beach area in question today. The time of the attack is uncertain, so we don't know if this new creature, or creatures, is—or are—limited by sunlight or not. See what you can find."

"Right." Buffy glanced at Oz. "Want to be my wheel man?"

"That would be a plan."

Buffy turned to Xander, who was clearly about to offer to go with them, catching him with mouth open and hand raised. "You want to cover the usual spots," she asked, "see if there's any new gossip?"

"Oooo, chatting with the undead. My favorite hobby. It's a little less effective when you don't have the Slayer with you, though."

"I'm sure you'll do fine," she said reassuringly. "Giles? You and Will going to keep up the research front?"

"Yes, I ah, I may know someone who may be able to help us. He's a herpetdemonologist, and—"

"Whoa." Xander made a time out gesture. "No fair using words with more than three syllables. Once again, in English?"

Giles sighed. "A scientist who specializes in the varieties of demons that live or hunt in water."

"Fun," Oz said with appreciation.

"You scare me with your ideas of fun," Xander told him seriously.

"So I'm Research Girl again?" said Willow, who was looking a little put-out at being stuck alone with book duty.

"Actually, until we have a little more information, a better place to start, I suspect that any research you do on this matter would be rather fruitless," Giles said. "However, we still need to put together the components of the changeling spell, and modify it to cleanse the skin, rather than attempt to fabricate a totally new spell. If Buffy is correct and this new creature is merely looking for Ariel, the sooner we have her ready to go, the better."

And with that, nobody could argue.

* * *

The day was quickly growing unseasonably warm, so by midmorning, Willow packed up her books and laptop. "Ariel? Come on, we're going outside."

Ariel blinked, then grinned a very human-kid grin. *"Amach?"* She added something that Willow guessed from the grin was the selkie equivalent of "Way cool!"

Settling herself, the books, and the laptop on a bench, Willow patted the bench to get Ariel to sit beside her, then took a deep breath of air that smelled kind of dry. Wind from the east. Ariel sniffed, too, and gave a little whimper, giving Willow a sad, worried glance.

"It's okay," Willow soothed. "You'll smell the ocean again, honest."

Ariel wriggled on the bench, pointing in sudden excitement. Wow, a *squirrel! Of course Ariel would find a squirrel exciting,* Willow thought. *Not too many squirrels in the ocean!*

It had been a good idea to come out here. She'd gotten pretty much all of the information available off the Net already, anyway, so now it was just a matter of fitting the pieces together.

Besides, Willow thought, watching Ariel watch the hyperactive squirrel running up and down a tree trunk, *she shouldn't be cooped up all day inside. Not good for any kid, certainly not one that's used to being outside all the time. Well, in the water, outside.*

"Hey there."

Willow looked up at the familiar voice, her stomach tightening at the thought of having to face Cordelia, even as another part of her brain informed her that a) Cordy wasn't using the particular voice she'd been using ever since she and Xander broke up, and b) it wasn't directed at Willow.

Ariel sat back on her heels, and looked up at Cordelia, her brown eyes curiously blank.

"Still hanging around this place, huh?" Cordy asked her, tucking her hair behind one ear and crouching down in front of the selkie. "Giles so needs to get a clue about child care—oh . . . Willow."

The tall brunette drew herself up and adjusted the strap of her Versace bag more securely over her shoulder.

"Cordelia." Willow was proud of the way her voice actually sounded welcoming. Well, she *did* like Cordy. Sometimes. Even when she was being the *uber*snob, it was tough to forget the fact that they'd actually been, well, friends.

Until you and Xander messed it up, she reminded herself.

"Giles actually let you out of that musty old library?" Cordy continued. "What's the occasion, National Dead Things and Demons Holiday?"

Not that Cordy doesn't have flaws of her own.

"I'm just working on a . . . special project," Willow replied, all her good intentions fading rapidly under Cordelia's look. "Nothing important."

Ariel chose that moment to investigate Willow's papers, and the redhead had to scramble to keep her printouts and Giles's neatly-written notes safe from grasping little hands.

"No, Ariel, bad girl, sit. Stay."

"She's not a dog, Willow. You can't just order her around like that."

"She's not exactly—well, she's not, um . . ."

For an instant, the look on Cordy's face changed into something almost . . . sympathetic. "Oh. Is she, you know, impaired?"

"No!" Willow's exasperation with Cordelia was quickly superseded by her irritation with the selkie. "Ariel, put that down!"

Ariel's attention span, fortunately, was about that of a three-year-old. She quickly lost interest in the papers she had dislodged and returned to stare at the tree, waiting for the squirrel to come back.

"No," Willow repeated, clutching her rescued papers. "Ariel isn't human, that's all."

Cordelia recoiled as if Willow had told her Ariel had head lice. "Oh."

"Hey! She's not a monster. Just a selkie, you know, a—a seal person. We're trying to find a way to get her back home."

Cordy's eyes widened. "You mean she's really a seal? She eats raw fish and things? That is so utterly gross."

"Hey, people do, too! You know, sushi?"

"And the *smell!*" Cordelia said over Willow's voice. "I mean, have you ever smelled the beach when the tide's going out? She lives in *that?*"

"Ariel does not smell! Come on, Cordelia, you thought she was kind of cute till now!"

"That was before I knew she isn't human."

"She won't hurt anyone. She's just a little girl!"

"Well, don't ask me to babysit, is all I'm saying. God, you people get involved in just the *weirdest* stuff."

Willow nodded, her gaze straying back to the papers scattered at her feet. "All right. We won't ask you for anything."

"Fine."

"Fine."

Then, as the brunette was walking away, Willow bit

her lip. If there really was something of the new and freaky in town . . .

"Cordelia?"

"What now?" She stopped and turned around, her body language screaming "get it out and get it over with."

"Be careful?"

The two girls looked at each other, both aware of the fact that being careful in Sunnydale meant much more than locking your doors and not talking to strangers.

"Always," was all Cordelia said.

"You're not much on beaches, huh?"

Buffy shook her head, sitting on the low wall that separated the beach from the road and looking out at the calmly rolling waves.

"Me neither," Oz admitted. His van was parked on the shoulder of the road a few yards away. The stretch of beach was gray and deserted, a far cry from the sun-drenched mythos of Southern California hedonism. "Guess that makes us odd."

Buffy laughed. She couldn't help it. "Oh, definitely. That's what makes us odd."

Standing up, she slipped off her shoes and wiggled her bare toes into the sand. It was cooler, more granular than she remembered from trips with her folks when she was younger. And when she got older, she'd preferred hanging out in the mall to sand and sweat.

And now . . . now relaxation was where she could grab it. No time for trips to the beach. Or the woods, or the desert, if she'd been so inclined. *Someday,* she thought, *I'm going to go hiking. Just to see if I like it.*

"So, what exactly are we looking for?" Oz asked.

"Haven't a clue," she replied lightly, her gaze taking in the wet sand down by the waterline. "Green-glowing slime? Weird-shaped footprints? Random body parts?"

"Right."

That was the great thing about talking to Oz. He made everything seem so . . . rational. Logical. Normal, even.

Neat trick, that.

"Uh . . . wait a minute." Oz was sniffing the air, frowning with concentration. Without another word to Buffy, he started down along the beach.

Geez, like a two-legged dog. Wolf. Whatever.

But sometimes his wolfiness did come in handy. Following, Buffy asked, "What?"

He dropped to hands and knees, still frowning.

If he puts his nose to the ground, Buffy thought, *I'm going to start giggling, I know it.*

"Willow," Oz said suddenly. "Definitely her. Ariel's scent, too, I think . . . No, more than that, maybe? More selkies, I guess. And—Whoa."

"Whoa what? Oz, what?"

He got back to his feet, the frown even deeper. "I don't know. Something really, really weird. Definitely not human. Not vampire, either. I've figured their smell by now. Don't recognize it at all—but there sure was a lot of it. Or them. And . . . I really don't know how to say this. But the scent is, well—hungry."

The vampire stopped short in the maze of Sunnydale's sewers, listening, head cocked to one side. Yes . . . that was definitely someone. Something. Not a rat or any other small life . . . not human, either. He had been a damn good hunter when he was alive, and what he was now complemented the old skills: He knew how to identify sounds.

And smells. The sewer reek didn't bother him—you got used to it, after a while. Being a demon didn't give you a lot of room to complain to management. But there was something sliding over the usual confusion of aromas: a hint of . . . salt. Ocean.

The vampire drew back his lips from his fangs in a silent snarl. He'd not been on the beach, but rumor had spread quickly. Something was killing humans—killing *his* rightful prey.

And now, whatever it was had discovered this closely-guarded route directly into the heart of Sunnydale—and the Hellmouth. He snarled again. It was bad enough that he had to share his hunting grounds with other vampires, as they all came to be close to the malignant warmth of the Hellmouth. But to have another predator sniffing around *their* meals . . .

Then he saw them, and for a fatal moment froze with utter surprise. Not human, not demon—what were these green-skinned, green-haired . . . things? Nothing he had encountered, not in sixty years of unlife, nor the thirty before then. They smelled strongly of blood, fresh-spilled, of healthy flesh and overlaying that, of the open sea—

And then the things were upon him, and the vampire had time for two quick thoughts: The creatures, whatever they were, had fangs sharp as his own, and they *hurt!*

He fell under their assault, slipping in the sludgy water underfoot, a hollow, whistling scream rising from his throat as he felt chunks of skin and muscle being torn from his body. Not even dying had hurt this much, not even dying had gone on for so long . . .

And then they dropped him, splashing facedown into the soiled water, listening uncomprehendingly to the angry, high-pitched chitter of his attackers.

The angry merrows, disgusted that what they had assumed was easy human prey wasn't, never saw the second vampire slipping warily away.

She, too, had heard the rumors. But she was older and slightly wiser than the first vampire, a reviewer who had cut short careers the way she now cut short lives, and she knew when she was outgunned. She didn't have a chance. Not when there were that many of them. Others needed to know about this, that the rumors were, if anything, understating the danger.

There weren't too many things that could unite the vampires of Sunnydale. For that, one needed a Master, an incredibly strong vampire to force them into teamwork—

That, or the threat of something that did not fear a demon.

CHAPTER 6

Handle, turn. Water, on. Towel, ready. Buffy went through the routine mechanically, her eyes barely open and her body definitely not awake yet. The Slayer was off-duty, and sleepy teenager reigned.

Hanging her robe on the back of the door, she turned back to check the water temperature. The way she felt this morning, after a day and night spent scouring Sunnydale for some trace of what killed those kids, with nothing to show for it, nothing short of scalding was going to wake her up. If it wasn't for the fact that she'd agreed to have a mom-and-daughter bonding brunch thing, she would still be curled up in bed, head under the pillow, sleeping the sleep of the exhausted.

But a little more lack of sleep's an acceptable price to pay for Belgian waffles. Don't know what I'd do with lots of normal shut-eye time, anyway.

Opening the shower door allowed steam to rise up

and fill the room, raising both the temperature and the humidity level. Buffy's eyes opened a little more, waking up in anticipation of a nice, long hot shower.

Matter of fact, the only thing wrong with this morning's plan was that after those waffles and bacon and other sinful things, she faced another day of chasing people-eating sea-things.

Lucky Willow, who got to spend the day waiting for autopsy reports to get entered into the morgue database so she could grab them. Much safer than actually going to the morgue itself, which was fine once or twice, but the fifth time in as many months, the attendants started to ask questions. Besides, Willow got such a kick out of hacking their mainframe.

If that girl ever turns to a life of corporate crime, it's going to be our fault, Buffy thought muzzily. *I wonder if she'll cut us in for a percentage of the profit.*

Then all thoughts were cut off by the sound of water splashing hard against tiling, the feel of moisture against her face and arm as she stepped into the tub . . .

The water triggered a memory, the dream she had managed to forget on waking. A thousand sensations rushed her unprepared brain and knocked it sprawling.

Green surfaces, oddly lit, kind of wavering in front of her eyes. Sunlight, but cool, clammy. The smell of sweat and fear, the knowledge that she had failed. Again. That she hadn't learned anything, again. That people were going to die, because she hadn't learned . . . what? What was it she was supposed to know? What was she supposed to be doing?

Thrashing wildly, she chased after the knowledge . . .

And came back to herself, halfway into the shower, her skin damp from a cold sweat.

Turning off the water with a shaky hand, she quickly revised her plans for the day.

"So, dream. Bad dream." Buffy collapsed at the small table Giles used for eating, her fingernails unconsciously tapping out a staccato beat on the surface. She didn't even remember getting there, only that he'd opened the door, and she'd started talking, all in a rush. After trying to get a word in edgewise, he'd steered her to the kitchen where he'd been making breakfast, seated her at the table, and then put the kettle on for tea, the Rupert Giles cure-all.

She hated tea, especially the way he made it. But she sipped it anyway.

"I mean, this one was . . . it was bad, Giles. I remembered all of it this time, all the little details, the specifics—I'm really not into the whole drowning thing, even when it's not actually of the dead-making sort. And I know I'm babbling, so don't do that whole concerned face thing, okay?"

Giles, in the process of pouring himself another cup of tea, quickly rearranged his face into a more appropriately bland expression.

"Thank you. Okay." Buffy leaned forward in her chair, looking up at her Watcher with a frown. "It was different this time. I'm in a pool. I know it's a pool. But the water's salty, and someone's holding me down under the surface." Buffy frowned, then shivered.

"Someone you know?" Giles prodded gently.

"Nuh-uh. Demon-like hand, all scaly and hard. Or maybe someone who's not been using Palmolive when they do their dishes."

Her Watcher sat at the table across from her, sipping

his morning tea. "Scaled hands. We'll have to add that to the list of characteristics. It may narrow things down."

Buffy let out a sigh of relief. "So you believe me now, that it's a premonition-whatever dream?"

He sat at the table opposite her, placing the cup down in front of him. "As I said before, it doesn't match the usual parameters of either a premonition or a prophetic dream. It would be unusual for a true prophetic dream to continue past the time you became aware of the actual threat. The addition of salt water is interesting, in that before, the dream involved only ordinary water, yes?"

She nodded. "Yeah. No. Pool water. You know, chlorinated. I distinctly remember it leaving a bad taste in my mouth. And I—"

Giles held up a hand to stop her. "It is entirely possible that you had a premonition last night of danger coming from the sea, intensified by the knowledge of what happened on the beach two nights ago."

"Yeah, a little thing like four dead people and no clue about the killers."

"However," Giles continued, ignoring her outburst, "the fact that you were dreaming of pool water originally supports my theory that the origin of these dreams is your subconscious mind trying to deal with a burgeoning phobia about water—perfectly understandable, considering past circumstances, enhanced by recent events. There's no shame in being uncomfortable about something, Buffy."

"I don't have a phobia!" She sat back, preparing to sulk until he relented and took her more seriously.

Giles, clearly recognizing the signs from three years

of experience, was just as clearly about to change the subject to something she would feel more in control of—the creature from last night's patrol, perhaps—when a crash and thud came from the living room.

"Ariel, blast it—"

He shot through the open doorway faster than Buffy could remember seeing him move except when vampires were involved. Curious, she followed, only to see her Watcher on his hands and knees, removing Ariel from the insides of a cabinet by her legs.

"How many times have I told you? No! Stay out of there."

The selkie wriggled bonelessly out of his grip and looked up at him, her normally impassive expression transformed by a definite self-satisfied smirk.

And . . . the Slayer shivered, like something cold and slimy had just walked down her back. *The smell of salt, the cold, clammy feel of scales . . .*

"Sean nithe!" Ariel stated.

"Yes, I know they're old things," Giles retorted, getting from his knees to the sofa with a grunt, "which is precisely why I keep them in there, and why you shouldn't be touching them."

It had the sound of a familiar discussion, one that Giles didn't have a prayer of winning.

"Welcome to parenthood, Giles," Buffy said, her momentary unease washed away by her amusement. "You want, my mom could give you some helpful pointers . . ."

"No. Thank you," he said stiffly, the stuffy effect kind of ruined when Ariel decided to climb into his lap and hug him around the neck, her eyes big and trusting. It was just too cute.

Buffy felt a pang go through her that had nothing to do with her dream-induced wiggins. There was a time when she had done that. Crawled into her dad's lap and let him soothe away whatever was wrong.

But that was a long time ago. Bad things didn't go away because a deep, rumbly voice said everything was going to be okay.

Not even if that voice was Giles's.

Still, she had to admit, he did look good playing daddy.

"Looks like you've been cast in the role of papa seal stand-in."

"Ah, yes." He got up with difficulty, depositing Ariel on the sofa. "For some reason, she's rather focused in on me."

"You make her feel safe," Buffy said offhandedly, not willing to admit to similar feelings. "Maybe tweed feels like sealskin to her, or something."

She looked at Ariel, now happily making a nest for herself out of the blankets tossed on the sofa. There was still something, something about Ariel that was stuck in the back of her head . . .

Oh. Duh. Right.

"You said she speaks a kind of really old Irish language, right?"

"Gaelic, yes. But I can't seem to manage an accent that sounds familiar enough to her, and the version of Gaelic I know is hardly as old as that of her people. And Willow's best efforts have not turned up any sites that might be of use."

"Why not have Angel try to talk to her? I mean, he's old, he's Irish . . . maybe he can speak it better."

Her Watcher stiffened the moment she said Angel's

name. Then Buffy saw his shoulders loosen up again, slowly, as he considered what she'd just said.

"I suspect the selkie version faded from use long before Angel was born. But perhaps he might at least be able to manage a better inflection on words I haven't quite been able to manage. An excellent suggestion."

"Yeah, well, you haven't come up with anything for me to pound into dust—or water, in this case—so I've got to use the brains, I guess."

"And quite well done, too. Next time you see him, you might ask."

"Right. I'm supposed to meet up with him tonight. By which time, I hope, we'll know what's doing the beachside noshing?"

Now, why should she feel an urge to look at Ariel? The selkie looked back at her, all wide-eyed kid innocence.

Yeah, right.

Or maybe, yeah, right, no sarcasm about it?

Wish I knew. About me, too.

"Giles?"

"Hmmm?"

No. Maybe Giles is right. Maybe I'm just overreacting to everything water-related. I mean, he's Knowledge Guy. But I'm the one with the Slayer instincts, right?

Or maybe, Buffy stopped, trying to fight the thought, then finally let it in. *Maybe I'm just being jealous 'cause he and Will are spending so much time with Ariel. Maybe . . .* She winced. *Okay, painful honesty time—maybe you really do resent the fact that there's this cute little girl wrapping Giles—your Watcher— around her little finger?*

Jealous of a lost little kid? It wasn't a picture of herself Buffy liked visualizing.

"Never mind. It's nothing."

Once again, Julian Lee found himself on the beach. It was almost amusing, if one was fond of sick jokes. He had been too busy at a seminar upstate to be here when the teams had gone out. And so, he had missed his chance, missed the opportunity to, as the saying went, finally put his money where his mouth was.

And he had a great deal of both to wield, words and money alike.

Dr. Julian Lee, Ph.D. in marine biology. Attached to an internationally renowned institute. Founder of E.L.F., a statewide organization of environmental volunteers. A familiar name to readers of the more important conservationist magazines and journals, and gadfly to the senators and congressmen who voted against causes he took a stand for. A lone crusader against a danger of which the rest of the world stood ignorant.

A danger he was determined to eradicate, no matter the personal cost.

But, once again, he was too late.

He stood again on the sand and frowned at the gentle waves of the incoming tide. It was mocking him, somehow, its refusal to give up any useful information a slap in the face of his certainty.

I know they're there, though. No paranoia about it. They are waiting. Watching. Plotting.

Still, he needed proof. He was a scientist, not a witch hunter. To accuse without cause, to raise fear where there should only be concern wasn't his way.

The girl who had been assigned to be his liaison with

the local university had been much the same sort as the rescue workers: cheerful, clean, and obsessed with saving the environment. But she had academic credentials and, in all likelihood, a hefty student loan, to moderate her enthusiasm. She had been tracking the recoveries, from the time they were brought in for cleaning to the moment they were released back into the wild. Some remained, still too weak to be on their own. But no seals, suspicious or otherwise. In fact, no seals had been brought in at all. One elderly sea lion, his lungs compromised by the damage, who had already been taken to his new home at a local zoo, but no seals at all.

Almost as though they had been warned away . . .

Lee shook his head, ridding himself of those thoughts. The lack of official records didn't surprise him—selkies were a cunning race, and unlikely to be caught by slow-moving humans. No, those cursed creatures were in this town; he could feel it in every fiber of his body. And he would not allow them to spread their evil through another innocent seaside town. The legends that called them angels cast down from heaven were man's way of dealing with their duplicitous nature: the faces of angels, the eyes of wounded saints— and the very nature of devils.

Oh, how melodramatic. Lee mocked himself, self-aware enough to know how he would sound to someone else.

It was all true enough, though, melodrama aside. The selkies had no souls, no sense of morality. They played with humans, toyed with them, and then tore them apart emotionally for fun, like a cat with a mouse it had no desire to eat.

But there was nothing more to be done here. Not

right now, with the tide coming in. Returning to his car, Lee headed back to the Marine Research Facility, to meet with the remaining E.L.F. team leaders. Perhaps he would be able to open their bleeding hearts—

Stop that, he told himself, irritated with the streak of cynicism that had crept into his thoughts lately. He had founded E.L.F. out of those very same concerns, to give civilians a way to aid the creatures harmed by man's actions. And if these Greenpeace wannabees were a bit naive, a bit feckless, it wasn't the worst crime of which they could be accused.

Oh no. There was much worse in the world.

CHAPTER 7

They stalked silently down the dark tunnel of the human town, greenish lips curled up in disgust, revealing glinting white fangs.

"*They are foulness,*" one merrow hissed in the silent speech.

"*Not so foul that you do not like their taste,*" their leader snarled back.

"*But this . . . this . . .*" and it made a gesture with one scaled arm, indicating the dripping walls and standing puddles of refuse.

"*They live on dryness, without the currents to sweep their filth away. They must make their own currents, dig tunnels like this to send their wastes from their living spaces.*"

"*And into our home,*" another merrow continued bitterly, "*into our mother ocean.*"

A bitter growl of agreement responded from the

other merrows in the pack. The promise of sweet-tasting human flesh had gotten them here. But the longer they thought on it, the more their hatred for the land-dwelling humans grew. And they knew only one way to deal with their anger: to savage their enemy, to bring it down and tear it into mouth-filling bits.

The lead merrow snarled them into silence. A frenzied pack was an unmanageable one. And it had not brought them here only to have them fall into hunger-madness.

"It is only right, then, only justice, that we reach them through their own waste-tunnels, and avenge the sea. Avenge ourselves."

The merrows chuckled silently at that. *"Oh yes, avengers,"* one purred. *"We are avengers."*

"But," one of them said, *"avengers or no—we hunger. And others—the ones of unliving flesh—feed on the humans as well!"*

"We will eradicate them as we have others who interfered in the past," the leader promised. *"And then, then we shall feast. Nothing can stand between us and our prey."*

"No!"

That would *be the one English word Ariel had learned,* Willow thought. "We're not going to hurt the skin, honest."

"But we can't test our spell without it," Giles added, a little more impatiently. His hair was standing straight up, like he'd been running his hands through it for several hours. Which, in fact, he had.

"No!"

The selkie clutched the skin to her chest, her eyes

wide with terror. Willow and Giles exchanged helpless glances, then Giles looked at his notes again. Pushing his glasses back up on his nose, he said, "I suppose we could try it without the skin. This variant of the spell doesn't specifically call for contact. All right then, Ariel, child, go sit down. That's right. Sit. Out of our way. Willow, if you would begin . . ."

The spell was a patchwork of several spells that almost but didn't quite do what they wanted. Giles hadn't wanted to improvise like that, but Willow had pointed out that they didn't have much choice.

Only now, when it was time to actually do it, Willow wasn't sure she'd gotten it right. She had rehearsed the mixture of English and Gaelic words carefully, but now she was sure she was going to goof up the pronunciation of something—

She swallowed hard, and forced herself to center and calm down. No. That was the worst way to begin a spell, convincing yourself it was going to fail. She inhaled, then exhaled again, feeling her heart rate steady out. *Okay.*

Voice steady, Willow began, *"Tonnadh, bochna,* wave, ocean, we call to you . . ."

Something was happening already, she was sure of it. A spell that old was bound to be potent.

" . . . your child, return her to your realm . . ."

Prickles were running up and down her spine. Yep, magic, happening here and now. *Major* rush.

"Bochna hear us, *bochna* heed us, heal your child, heal your child, heal your child!"

Ariel stood up, her brown eyes wide, her nose practically twitching in excitement.

The words echoed within the library, the pressure building and pressing against their inner ears.

And . . .

"Nothing!" Willow wailed, feeling the pressure subside.

Giles let out his breath in a long sigh. "Nothing," he agreed. "There was a momentary gathering of power—you felt it, yes?—but I'm afraid it wasn't strong enough to be usable. A failure."

"Uh . . . Giles . . . ?" Willow held up a leafy little branch. "Where . . . did this . . . oh."

Giles blinked. "A pencil," he said, frowning at it. "Or rather, it *was* a pencil."

Willow and he stared at each other for an instant, then both of them started busily making notes.

Meanwhile, Ariel sat down on the floor with a dejected and vaguely disgusted *"harumph."*

"Well," Xander began as he and Buffy stepped out again onto Sunnydale's main street in the late afternoon. "A little more success with the Slayer along for the Q&A session. So far we've found out that aliens visited Mrs. Green to discuss her knitting, Good Ole Bob caught himself a talking fish after hitting a bottle of Good Ole High Test, and—"

"Xander."

"Right. One last stop, and we'll hit the Espresso Pump for a couple of extreme caffeines to celebrate a total waste of an afternoon before reporting in."

"Not a waste yet," Buffy said grimly. "Somehow, I suspect our last visit will pay off."

Xander rubbed his hands together in anticipation. "Oooooo. Do I get to be bad cop this time? If you're nice, it'll confuse the heck out of him, I bet."

Buffy snorted, and led the way on to Willy's Bar.

The interior was dark and cool, and Buffy could feel the sweat on the back of her neck drying almost instantly.

Willy looked up as they entered, and the half-smile left his face as he saw the two of them. "Not again." He leaned over to hit a small bell on the bar, and half the room got up and shuffled out the back entrance. Not all of them were vampires, either. Buffy didn't even spare them a glance. She'd deal with them later. Eventually.

"Hello, Willy," she said in her most charming voice, giving him the benefit of full Slayer perkiness.

"I don't know anything."

"About?"

"Anything. Blank slate, that's me."

Xander sneered. "Yeah. Sure. Maybe we should, you know, prod your mind a little?"

Willy glanced at Buffy. "He been watching cop movies, right? Lemme guess—you're the good cop?"

Buffy opened her mouth, shut it, caught a glimpse of Xander's insulted face, and laughed in spite of herself. "Listen, Willy, I'm not in the mood to play. So let's pretend I've already thrown you around a bit, and you can just cut to the chase."

Buffy stormed into Giles's house as soon as he opened the door, and flung herself down on the sofa, then sprang up again as she realized she'd just sat on a book, shoved it aside, and slumped down again.

"Good afternoon to you, too," Giles called over his shoulder as he returned to the table where he was working on a bunch of spread-out papers.

"Sorry. Annoyance, extreme. Xander and I just spent all day hunting down every possible rumor of weirdness in all of Sunnydale. Do you know how many rumors that is in this town?"

"A lot?" Willow suggested wearily, pausing with an armful of what looked like parchment scrolls.

"You got it! And you know what we found? Nothing! No hints, no leads, not even a tip from Willy."

"Xander didn't, uh, I mean, not again?"

"No violence, Will. Well, maybe threat of. But nothing nada zip. And no, Willy wasn't faking. He really didn't know a thing. Half his clientele's not showing up, and the ones who do aren't talking, either."

"Our day was pretty much a bust, too," Willow said with a sigh, putting the scrolls down on a pile of books. Moving another pile of books off a chair, she flopped down on the seat.

"Didn't *anything* work?" Buffy asked.

"We haven't had the selkie skin for very long," Giles reminded them, balancing an awkward pile of books in his arms.

Buffy jumped up to catch the top book before it could slither out of his grasp. He thanked her with a nod, lowered the pile to the floor, and sat down with a sigh of relief on the one free chair.

"Granted, none of the simpler spells seems to have any effect at all, but we have barely, uh, scratched the surface."

"Well, we can't keep her here forever," Buffy said flatly, reclaiming her seat. "She's putting a severe cramp in your Watcherly behavior."

"Buffy, what *is* the matter with you? Regardless of her species, Ariel is just a child."

Ariel, who'd been curled up out of sight against the side of a chair, raised her head with an inquiring little whine at the sound of her name. Her eyes were dimmed, not as wet-shiny as they'd been even yesterday, but that could have just been because she was sleepy.

Buffy let out a heavy breath, aware that she wasn't exactly being rational about all this, but unable to stop the words from coming out of her mouth. "Yeah, a selkie child. Right. Whose folks haven't done much about even looking for her."

"Buffy!" Willow said.

The Slayer glared at her best friend. "Well? They haven't exactly been beating down Giles's door, have they? They're the ones who got her lost, not us. They're the ones who should be worrying about her, not us. We've got other things, more important stuff to be spending time on."

Willow just looked hurt at the suggestion that they weren't doing as much to help Buffy as they should, while Giles's frown deepened. "I'm beginning to wonder exactly why it is that you dislike Ariel."

"I . . . don't . . ."

"She needs our help to get home," Willow said indignantly. "Come on, Buffy, she's one of the good guys. You know, lives peaceably with her neighbors, doesn't eat people or cast nasty spells, or anything like that. Oh. No, you can't really believe that story, you know, the one Xander found, that said selkies were angels that got cast into the sea for rebelling against God? That they were, you know, soulless, like demons?"

"Hey. Hellmouth. I try not to discount anything of the weirdness anymore. Isn't that what you're always trying to drum into my skull?"

Giles sighed. "There is nothing demonic *or* angelic

about selkies. They are mortal creatures, as much a part of the ecosystem as humanity—perhaps more so."

"Yeah," Buffy said dryly, "and besides, seal pups are cute."

"Indeed they are. And I am not mistaking Ariel for a human girl, believe me. She is very much the wild creature." Giles snorted. "Charming though the child may be, I'm getting very weary of finding my belongings broken, misfiled, or out-and-out lost!"

"Ok. Seal. Pup. Kid. Whatever. Right. I know." Buffy put a firm hold on her paranoia. "I'm sorry. Just ignore me and my bad case of the getting-nowheres. You know I get cranky when I can't slay something."

Willow smiled at her, all forgiven. Giles watched her for a moment longer, then went back to his reading.

Buffy glanced back over her shoulder at Ariel, who stared right back at her. Those large, dark eyes were suddenly totally unreadable.

Totally alien.

Totally wigging her out.

The mobile lab wasn't the height of modern technology, but it served its purpose well enough: to house biologists working on emergency sites, in the aftermath of disasters natural or manmade, or where there was no access to better, more permanent laboratory space. The Institute had three, none of which could be taken out of the storage garage without high level permission, in triplicate, on two different forms.

At the moment, the oversized van covering the *Roxanne* spill cleanup was parked in the back of a Motel 6 in the late afternoon shadows, the computers shut down and the equipment and medical supplies locked in their bins and cabinets. The only light came from one small modular desk snuggled up against the far wall.

Dr. Lee was seated at that desk, comparing the long printout he had taken from the Marine Facility to a small notebook filled with his own scrawled notes.

"This can't be right," he muttered. "Every report I've gotten indicates the presence of a colony here. They couldn't have escaped, not all of them."

On the desk beside him, newspaper clippings spilled from a plain green folder. Lurid headlines like "Girl, 20, Dies in Drowning Accident," and "Man Drowns Children, Self," made an odd contrast to the stark, scientific atmosphere. The clippings were highlighted in places with yellow marker and red pen, and Lee touched the folder every now and then, absently, as a preacher might caress his Bible, or a hunter pet his favorite dog.

But . . . this printout . . . this maddening printout . . .

"No, no, no . . . dammit!"

Frustrated, Lee threw the printout onto the desk, hand raised as though about to strike someone—

Control, he snapped at himself. *Control.*

Slowly lowering his hand again, Lee forced himself to breathe normally until the flare of anger passed.

"Dr. Lee?"

A tousled blond head poked through the sliding door that separated the driver's cab from the rest of the lab. "Is something wrong?"

Control, Lee reminded himself yet again, and smiled, shaking his head. "Nothing, Ritchie. Just me being frustrated. It seems that no matter how well we think we're doing, there are always too many who slip through our fingers."

Ritchie nodded, knowingly. "Yeah, I know. It gets personal."

Oh, you have no idea, Lee thought, as his grad student/aide waved goodnight and left the van for his room in the motel that was their home for the duration. *You have no idea at all how personal it can get . . .*

And I pray that you never do.

CHAPTER 8

The vampire stirred, struggling out of unconsciousness, blinking eyelids that didn't want to open. In life, she had been wiry and lean, an Olympic hopeful gymnast. Now she kept a hint of her old grace as she sat up, one leg curled under so that she could spring to her feet, listening and scenting the rank air. Nearby, she could sense and scent other vampires resting, at unspoken truce during daylight hours, waiting for the night that was almost here.

There was comfort in gathering this way, although they would hunt alone, come full night. But when the burning sun ruled, they came to this place, taking some measure of comfort from the heavy walls and doors of the abandoned and forgotten sewage reclamation station.

Daylight. She hissed, stretching. Overhead, outside, the sun was beginning to set. But she could still feel it, through her skin, scorching her blood. It was safe here, though. Smelly, ugly, but dark. Never a chance of any stray beams to hit—

She stopped, midstretch, her predator's senses alert to something very wrong.

Noise, a faint aroma, something creeping along the walls, disturbing the currents of water that ran through the sewers just below them. Something alive. Something that wasn't supposed to be there.

"Trouble!" she yelled, jumping up, then stumbling over another vampire crashed on a pallet at her feet.

She recovered only in time to see a dozen or so shapes rushing into the room, overwhelming the nest. The other vampires staggered to their feet, only dimly realizing what was happening before the strangers were upon them. Fangs flashed, claws tore, green merrow blood and red vampire blood flowed, looking black in the dim light. No one screamed or shouted, they simply snarled, and kicked, and bit.

And died.

For some, the first time. For others, again.

The air felt nice, cool, but not cold, and Willow lifted her face to catch the evening breeze. It was so rare, now, to sit outside, even at dusk, and just enjoy. But the front door to Buffy's house was open, in case they had to scramble, and the porch light was set to go on automatically, the minute it got to a certain level of being dark. The minute it went on, they'd go inside.

Besides, she wasn't out here alone. Buffy's mom was just inside, doing paperwork at the dining room table, and Buffy was right there, playing catch with Ariel, trying to tire her out so they could drop her back at Giles's.

"Hey."

Willow jumped, the stake by her side up and aimed, then looked at Angel reproachfully. "Bells! Chimes! Something, okay?"

"Sorry."

Buffy appeared by their side, leaving Ariel momentarily occupied with the texture of a tree's trunk. "Hey. You're early." And then to her friend, "Will, that kid's a menace. She's got more energy than, well, something with a lot of energy. I don't know how Giles does it."

"With a lot of muttering," Willow said, and Buffy smothered a grin of agreement. Her Watcher had been doing more than muttering when she'd left the apartment. He'd even admitted—he who almost never confessed true frustration—that his temper had just about reached the last measure when Ariel decided that it would be fun to make the tub overflow. He'd looked pretty frayed, Buffy had noted. That was the only reason she'd agreed to take on the selkie for a few hours before patrol.

And, to her surprise, it was nice just to sit for a minute, tossing a ball around, or watching Ariel try to catch a squirrel.

That's more her speed, I guess.

Dogs, the selkie shied away from, and after getting her nose scratched by a feline who didn't appreciate small hands tugging at his fur, she'd avoided cats as well. But squirrels—small, fuzzy, and uncatchable—were deeply fascinating.

"Who's the kid?" Angel asked, breaking into her musing.

"Ariel. Resident selkie, remember?"

"She's the selkie?" Angel looked at Ariel with re-

newed interest, clearly distracted from what had brought him there to stand in the shadows. "Never thought I'd actually see one."

"Congratulations," she said dryly. "Scratch another supposedly mythological creature off the 'doesn't exist' list. At this rate, I fully expect to see leprechauns dancing down the street next Saint Patrick's day. And what makes it worse," she continued, working up a good head of steam the more she thought about it, "is that they're all determined to make Sunnydale their hot vacation spot, thereby making my life even more impossible. What's with that, anyway? Doesn't the Hellmouth have some kind of crowd limit or something?"

Angel frowned, concentrating his senses on Ariel instead of the familiar Buffy-rant. "She doesn't seem like a threat."

"Oh, not her. She's, like, the one nonthreatening thing around." Buffy smirked slightly. "Although I bet Giles would say different. He dumped her on us so he could sealproof his house. Which reminds me, how's your Gaelic?"

"My Gae—passable, at best. Why?"

"That's all Ariel speaks," Willow said, "some kind of old version of it, Giles says, and his accent's really bad."

Buffy nodded. "We were kind of hoping you'd be able to do the translating thing. While we're waiting for some kind of update on the dead bodies. Will says they haven't gotten around to putting the autopsy reports in the central database yet, 'cause of last month's wave of business, and we're at a total standstill on the getting new information front."

Angel shook his head. "Sorry. What little I did

know . . . long gone. Not much call for it over the years."

"Nothing's ever easy," Willow sighed, then raised her voice. "Ariel! No! Away from the road!"

The selkie stopped on hearing her name, although she clearly didn't understand anything else. "Ariel, no!" Willow repeated, and made a 'come here' gesture.

The selkie looked longingly at the squirrel now safely on the other side of the road, then shrugged and came back into the yard. As she got closer, Angel studied her with more interest.

"Interesting."

"What is?"

"What?" The vampire seemed surprised that he had spoken out loud. "Oh, nothing. I just . . . her blood. Everything else about her feels human, but her blood . . . smells different."

"Different how?" Willow asked, curious.

"Unappetizing."

"Well. That's nice to know," Buffy said dryly. "Think we can bottle that and sell it like perfume? Because I could fund my college education with that."

"Mine, too," Willow said fervently. " 'Eau de Night,' for when you have to be out after dark. We'd make a fortune."

"Down, girl," Buffy said, shaking her head at the predatory gleam in her friend's eye. "Speaking of smelling . . . and on the subject of the dead bodies, Oz said he smelled something on the beach. I mean, besides usual beach stuff. And Willow. Whom he homed in on like a bloodhound, by the way. You ever change perfume, Will, you're going to have one very confused wolf-boy on your hands."

"It's not my perfume he smells," Willow said. "It's emotions. You know, the way you sweat more, when you're scared? Or something like that."

"Oh?" Buffy was diverted for a moment. "We're going to discuss that later, girlfriend. Giles'll want to test that, see if it's just you, or if he can track any of us like that."

"A strange smell?" Angel said, taking pity on Willow, who looked horrified at the idea of being a lab rat.

"Oh, yeah. Something weird, and fishy and . . . he said it smelled hungry. Does that make any sense? Can something smell hungry?"

The vampire shrugged. "Fear has a smell, so does lust. It makes sense that hunger would, as well."

Lust? Okay, topic we don't want to go into, Buffy thought. He still wasn't much on the open sharing of talk, but she'd learned how to read him pretty well. Especially when the subject got off-limits.

"So I keep thinking," Buffy said instead, watching as Willow tried to coax Ariel away from the road again, "that somehow Ariel's mixed up in the dead bodies thing."

Angel glanced at Ariel, then stared at Buffy in disbelief. "The selkie? Why would you think that?"

"Hello? Am I the only one who sees a pattern here? You know, selkie arrives, dead bodies show up, all on same stretch of beach, within twenty-four hours of each other? Oddness, just a little?"

Ignore the whole maybe-jealous thing. The fact that just being around her's making me cranky may not be the norm for identifying creatures of the night, but it says maybe something's off kilter!

"Selkies are—"

"Yeah, I know," Buffy cut in, "remarkably nonviolent, except when it comes to fish. They fall in love with humans, but're lousy at long-term relationships, and they're reputed to both help and hinder fishermen, depending on who you ask. I've been over this ground with Willow and Giles, both of whom think Ariel's just the neatest thing to hit the ground since the printing press. But . . . I keep having these dreams . . ." She hadn't told him any of this. Hadn't wanted to tell him about this. Telling Giles had been tough enough, and it was Giles's job to know about these things, tell her what to worry about, what not to. But Giles could take care of the weirdness factor—he couldn't make her insides feel safe.

She took a deep breath, caught Angel's sympathetic gaze, and plunged on. "I keep dreaming I'm drowning, that someone's holding me under water. And it started out as in a pool, and then a shallow tub, kind of, so flashbacks, right? But then it changed . . . to salt water . . ."

"So you're picking up on something coming in from the ocean, maybe to do with the oil spill. But why do you think Ariel's involved?"

Buffy took a deep breath, then let it out. "Because I look at her, and I think 'oh, cute.' And then I look at her again, and . . . and it's 'not cute, dangerous.' "

"Of course you do," Angel said reasonably.

"What?"

"Selkies aren't human, Buffy. You're designed to protect humans. So she's bound to set off some kind of alarm system. And . . . "

"Spit it out," Buffy demanded, when he seemed on the verge of shutting down again. "And what?"

"And you said it yourself—both Willow and Giles are taken with her."

"You're saying I'm reacting that way because I'm jealous?"

"Well?"

It jibed way too well with what she'd been trying to deny. "Okay. Maybe. A little. A very little. But I like your first answer better."

"Buffy!"

Willow's scream had them both in motion before she hit the second syllable. On the sidewalk, Willow was scrambling backward with Ariel in her arms, as a vampire crawled out from beneath a sewer cover.

Male, medium build, Buffy categorized in her mind even as she went on the offensive. Something else nagged at her, but not enough to slow the rush of her attack. An upward shove to the jaw got him off-balance, and he staggered back into the street. She followed through with the heel of her palm to his gut, and he doubled over, falling to his knees just in time for her stake to sweep downward and impale him from behind.

"Thanks," Willow said, collapsing on the sidewalk with Ariel in her lap, clinging to her, wide-eyed.

The porch light came on just then, and everybody jumped. "Buffy . . . ?" Joyce called from inside the house. "Everything all right?"

"Yeah, Mom. No prob," Buffy added to Willow, the niggling thing finally getting a chance to come to the fore. "He was in lousy shape. Did you see? Missing an ear, part of a hand—like someone'd already been chewing on him."

She turned to look at Angel, who had stayed out of this simple fight. "If you know where you're going, you can get to the ocean through the sewers." It wasn't a question.

"Yeah."

"Oh," Willow said. "Bad thing. You think maybe he tangled with Oz's hungry something-or-other?"

"That's what we're going to find out," Buffy declared. "Will, get Ariel inside. Call Giles, tell him we're on the case."

She looked down into the open sewer and wrinkled her nose in disgust. "Why can't anything ever lurk in, say, movie theaters? Nice, dry, comfortable, clean-smelling theaters, so I can catch something before it's been on cable for a month?"

"That would never work," Angel said. As Buffy glanced at him, puzzled, he added, absolutely deadpan, "The popcorn would get caught in their teeth."

CHAPTER 9

Buffy made a face and—for half a fleeting second—envied the vampire walking beside her. Breathing was definitely a hindrance down here in Sunnydale's sewers. Even if you got used to the slimy feel of everything, and the weird lighting of the yellow safety lights, the smell still rated a severe *yech*.

"Why does so much of my life revolve around things that are totally disgusting?" she grumbled. "Who took a vote on this? 'Cause if I ever find out who made that rule, I'm going to get medieval on their butts."

Angel, wisely, didn't respond. She had been venting all night, working herself into a state of righteous indignation that didn't bode well for anything even vaguely aggressive they found down here tonight.

Walking side by side, they turned a narrow corner and looked down the tunnel. Angel let out a silent hiss of frustration. The tunnel ran maybe another ten feet before branching off into two equally unappealing choices. He glanced at Buffy, who shrugged. They slogged forward, starting to lose a little of their alertness under the unending sameness of it all, until they came to where the tunnel forked.

"Which one?" Buffy asked. "Flip a coin? Toss a stake? I know, let's go to the left."

"Any particular reason?"

"Nope. Just a total whim on my part. You have a better suggestion?"

Angel sniffed the rank air, then shook his head. "No. I thought I smelled saltwater, but the air's filled with the tang of metal from the new sewer pipes they were installing last week."

"Great. Trust Sunnydale to have civic pride at exactly the wrong time."

"We could cover more ground if we split up, each take one," he suggested reasonably.

"We could," she agreed. But neither one of them made a move to split up.

Five minutes later, Buffy was just about to suggest that they turn back and go right instead. The tunnel was starting to close in on her, and if she was beginning to feel claustrophobic, she could only imagine how the much-taller Angel was reacting.

"Nothing down here," he said, before she could suggest going back. "That's new."

"Yeah." Now that he mentioned it, it really was quieter than usual. "Not even that little scurry-squeak of rats. Not that I'm complaining, mind you." She slipped a little in the ankle-high water, and cursed under her breath, words her mother would have been very unhappy about.

Angel stopped to lend her a hand, then froze, head raised and eyes glinting sharply in the faint light. He moved silently forward, and Buffy followed warily. They came out into a widening of the sewer tunnel, maybe ten feet wide and thirty feet long. Better, but still not the best place for a battle, which was what Angel stopping like that usually meant.

"Look." His voice sounded funny. Not alarmed, but not "not worried," either.

Buffy stalked forward, stake ready in her hand. The nearest body stirred at her approach, but was unable to do more than glare at her. "Vampires. Of the very damaged kind. Aw, someone took all the fun out of my job."

There were maybe a dozen bodies, half-covered in the sludge that ran along the tunnel floor. All of them lay face-up, huge gouges on their bodies—

Like a shark took chunks out of them, Buffy thought uneasily. But unlike the humans found on the beach, these were still aware, their undead bodies unable to give up the ghost, so to speak, despite the damage inflicted.

It was a kind of Slayer's buffet: downed vamps, no waiting. But Buffy didn't feel the usual rush of energy that came when given the chance to take out a bunch of demons. Something didn't feel right. It was that ookiness from her dream, all over again. Nothing from the dream was actually here, except maybe it being damp beyond belief, but the feeling was the same.

Angel walked cautiously amid the mangled bodies, stopping every now and then to lift a body part out of the sludge and study it. "They didn't go down easily," he noted, side-stepping one of the more active ones who tried weakly to swipe at his leg.

"Or happily." Buffy followed his trail, staking each vamp corpse as soon as Angel nodded that his examination was done. An incapacitated vamp made for a happy Slayer, but a dusted one was even better. "But we still don't know what attacked them. Something that came from the sea, which makes sense. I should have thought of the sewer system way before. But there aren't any bodies other than these. No nonvamps."

"They carried off their dead or wounded," Angel murmured. "Whoever they are. That means some of whatever they are is still out there."

"Out there, or in here with us?"

"Good question. Wait here." And with that he disappeared farther down the tunnel, out of the dim light.

"Right. I'll just stay here and clean up a little." She went on with the dusting, a series of perfectly executed moves that would have made her Watcher's heart proud.

She yawned, making a production of it. "Boring . . ." But the uneasy feeling remained.

Angel returned just as she was finishing up the last of the baker's dozen corpses. "Looks like whoever—or whatever—it was has long gone. Too bad there's so much," and he gestured distastefully at the watery sludge at their feet. "Washed away any evidence."

"No, not all," Buffy said. She bent, holding her breath, and scooped up something slimy from where it had wrapped around her boot.

"Seaweed," Angel said dismissively.

"In the sewer? This far in? I don't think so." She looked more closely, running it through her fingers. "Angel, this is hair." Holding it up to what light there was, she added, "Extremely green hair."

CHAPTER 10

Buffy frowned at the closed library door, then looked up and down the hallway. Giles's idea of Watcher Security 101: You weren't allowed to lock the door during school hours, but a closed door and the CLOSED FOR RESHELVING sign usually kept someone from barging right in, and bought Giles a few precious seconds to hide—well, whatever they were up to at the moment.

Okay, now what spell are they trying in there?

She wasn't really in the mood to find out. She and Angel had spent all night down in the sewers, trying to find more evidence, and even scrubbing in the shower till her skin was sore hadn't made her feel really clean again. She'd managed to grab an hour or so of shut-eye after that, thankfully of the undreaming kind, which had helped more, but the Slayer-o-meter was redlining in the foul mood zone.

But it wasn't a total waste of an evening. A lot fewer

vamps to deal with, for one thing. And there was that eerie clump of hair . . .

Angel hadn't been convinced it *was* hair, much less that it belonged to their mystery monster. But hair was something she knew way better than any guy, dead or alive. *So let's see what Giles makes of it.*

She entered the library, warily closing the door behind her again, just in time to hear Willow, huddled over something on one of the tables, say in alarm to Oz, "Careful . . . just don't . . . oh!"

There was a small but undeniable "bang," and a cloud of sour-smelling smoke drifted toward Buffy. She wrinkled up her nose. Great. Another reek. "Not going to win any perfume company contracts with that one, guys."

Willow gave her friend a reproachful look. Giles coughed a little into a handkerchief, then assured the fledgling witch, "Never mind. We haven't run out of combinations yet."

"No luck yet, I take it."

"Nope," Oz said tersely. His hair was blond this morning. Buffy frowned. Hadn't it been a sort of orange-y yesterday? He saw her looking and shrugged. "One of the spells that kinda misfired."

"You mean that's your natural hair color?"

Oz looked puzzled for a moment. "Y'know, I don't really remember."

Buffy moved forward to look over Willow's shoulder. "Swiped stuff from the chem lab?"

"I didn't swipe it," Willow said indignantly. "I told them I needed it for, well, homework."

"Work, it most certainly is," Giles noted, jotting the results down in a notebook. "I only wish we could do this at home, but the sight of us leaving school grounds with so many chemicals would give Snyder something to yip at us about."

"Calling our principal a small dog?" Xander asked.

"I would call him worse, if I weren't required to act as a role model for all of you," Giles said testily. He and Snyder'd had a run-in last week about some of the books Giles had ordered, Buffy remembered. She'd missed it, but Willow had been in shock for hours afterward, and Xander had looked *really* impressed.

"Okay. I think I know where we went wrong that time," Willow said. "We were using three pinches of dried vervain, only that's for inner cleansing, not outer. Not outer selkie, anyhow. Maybe if we try rosemary *and* vervain . . ."

Buffy opened her mouth to say something about her findings, but the argument that broke out between Giles and Willow over sea-based magicks—salt as the spell base, versus landed magicks—typically an herbal base, suggested that she wasn't going to get a word in edgewise any time soon.

Great. "Wiccan Debate Turns Ugly, Tonight on the Ten O'clock News."

She glanced at Ariel, curled up asleep in a chair, oblivious to the furor around—and because of—her. The little girl had lost weight in just the few days since her arrival; her cheekbones were way more pronounced, her skin dryer, almost flaky-looking. Cordelia would have prescribed moisturizer, and some regimen of vitamins and exercise, no doubt. But to Buffy's eyes, Ariel just looked . . . tired. Worn out.

Man, I can so relate.

Then Ariel woke up, her eyes opening and focusing

on Buffy's face, and the little shiver that never quite went away when Ariel was around slithered down her spine again. If only the selkie looked a little less human—maybe if she had gills or something, the sense of weirdness wouldn't bother Buffy so much. But seals—and selkies—were mammals. No gills, no fins, no nothing. No way to tell just from looking at her that Ariel wasn't just a kind of weird-looking kid. If Willow hadn't sensed the magic around her, she would probably just have been dumped at the hospital, and never gotten home.

Irritated at her inability to just accept the selkie the way the others had, Buffy turned to her Watcher. Time to reassert priorities here.

"Giles, I hate to break into this magical recipe exchange here, but I've got something on our other little problem to re—"

But just then someone rapped on the library door. Ariel came out of the chair with wild animal swiftness, reaching for Giles with a panicky whine. "In my office," he told her, gesturing, and she shot inside. As he closed the door behind her, Giles said to the startled others, "Can't be too careful."

"People starting to wonder why she's not in school?" Buffy asked.

"Not yet, but I see no reason to expose her more than necessary. Enter!" he called belatedly.

The man who entered was, Buffy guessed, somewhere around Giles's age, though it was tough to tell: He had the sort of face that always looked grim. *He could have been a honey, too,* Buffy thought, *for an older guy, anyway, with those dark, oval-shaped eyes and the elegant streaks of gray in his straight black hair.* But the bitter set to his mouth spoiled the effect. It was an expression that made her very wary. People who looked like that generally had 'tudes that made everyone else unhappy, too.

Willow didn't seem to be worried. Grinning, she got to her feet. "Dr. Lee! It's good to see you again! You know," she added, a little deflated when he stared blankly, "E.L.F.? Emergency Local Force? You came by and talked to us, back in June?"

The set of the grim mouth eased ever so slightly. "Ah. Of course. Forgive me; I speak to many groups, and I'm afraid they do tend to run together after a while." Turning to the others, he said, almost smiling, "I am Dr. Julian Lee, and as the young lady has already mentioned, I am affiliated with the local group trying to contain the oil slick's damage.

"In fact," Dr. Lee continued to Giles, "I'm staying on in Sunnydale to make sure that the effects of the oil slick have been completely cleaned up."

Giles frowned slightly. "That's quite a commendable goal, but I don't quite understand why you've come here. This is, after all, a high school library."

"Yes. I was hoping I could find . . ." He paused. "I need to check news articles about the pinniped population of the local coastline, for the past few decades."

"Pinni—?"

Lee turned to look at Buffy. "Sea mammals, such as seals and sea lions. There are a few anomalies I've spotted in the social patterns of the herds I've observed, and I need to confirm my findings."

"Here?" Xander was frankly incredulous. "What's wrong with the public library?"

Dr. Lee hesitated, as though trying to find the best

way to say something distasteful. "I'm afraid . . . the public library, while housed in a lovely building, is not quite up to a serious researcher's standards. And the newspaper's own archives, while complete, take forever to requisition. I spoke with a young woman at the library, and she suggested that I try here. Apparently the high school's library is rather well known for the unusual amount of information stored here."

"Ah." Giles was flustered, but pleased. "Of course. Let me check our database, and we'll see what we have that can help." Giles deftly maneuvered Dr. Lee over to the terminal he'd been forced to use—well away from the mess of spell components still lying there—and hesitated over the keyboard until he remembered the right combination of keys to press.

As the two men studied the resulting display, Buffy whispered to Willow, "Something's weird. Okay, I mean, we know Giles has got like everything ever written down stored here, but why's this guy in such a rush to get that information? And information about seals, especially?"

Willow's eyes widened. "Ariel? You think he's—"

"Shh! I don't know. I don't *think* he's anything other than human, anyway."

Where else but in Sunnydale could you say something like that, and mean it?

"He has to be human!" Willow protested. "He—he's a biologist! He helps out on things like the oil spill!"

And that automatically makes him a good guy.

But Buffy didn't say that. In fact, she didn't say anything, just watched Dr. Lee as though she wasn't at all interested in what he was doing. He seemed to be genuinely intrigued by the material Giles was now showing him, and Buffy caught snatches of, "typical harbor seal behavior," and "seal or sea lion?"

Yet all the while, she could have sworn Dr. Lee had his mind on something other than the papers Giles was showing him. It was weird, like he had eyes in the back of his head, or an inner antenna kind of like her own, homing in on whatever it was he was really here for.

Still, whatever, it wasn't strong enough to let him zero in on Ariel or her coat, which—*ohmigod*—was still on the table!

Not good. Really, really, really not good . . .

She made frantic eyes at Oz, who was still standing by the table. He frowned, then looked down to where his hand rested. Comprehension dawned.

Moving casually, he sat down and flipped open one of the books Willow had been consulting, drawing Giles's notebook closer in as though continuing a research project. As he did so, he managed to slide the heavy coat off the table and onto his knees, so that it was half-hidden by the table.

Not perfect, but it'll have to do.

"You were right," Dr. Lee was saying regretfully to Giles. "I don't think there's anything for me here after all. Unless . . ."

He took a step toward Giles's office, as though just realizing that there might be more information stored there, but Willow leaped up to block his path.

"There's nothing in there," she babbled, "just, you know, books. Old books. Nothing you could use, honest."

Way to go, Will, Buffy thought. *That's really going to convince him we're not hiding anything.* "Come on, Will. You know there's the entire run of *Marine Life* from 1890 to 1910 in there." She gave Dr. Lee her most dazzling "I'm such a blonde!" smile. "That wouldn't be any good, would it? I mean, that was sooo long ago, it couldn't be important now!"

Her dippiness had shaken the smallest of smiles out of him. "No, my dear. Of course not." His bow took in all of them. "Sorry to have wasted everyone's time."

The library doors closed behind him with a final-sounding *snick*, and Lee mentally berated himself for allowing that tweedy librarian to hustle him out of there. They knew something, he could practically smell it in the air. The scent of secrecy, like a stink fouling his lungs.

When Ritchie had told him what he'd heard, about a young girl's sudden departure from the beach that morning of the cleanup, with someone—or something—clinging to her as she bicycled away . . . Easy enough to learn who the girl had been, easy enough to trace her whereabouts here. They'd been clever enough to leave no blatant clues in the library, and he could hardly have produced a search warrant. But after eleven long years of hunting, he knew what he knew.

They were hiding a selkie.

No matter. It won't be able to escape me for long.

Moving away from the doors, he almost bumped into a tall, leggy brunette coming down the hallway.

"Oh!"

"My apologies," he said, steadying her. "I'm afraid I wasn't looking where I was going."

"Escaping the library has that effect on people," the girl agreed. "Anywhere's usually better than hanging out in there."

Intrigued, he took another look at his companion. An ally, perhaps? Yes, perhaps, if handled properly . . .

"You sound as though you've had a run-in or two with the librarian, Mr. . . ."

"Giles," she supplied quickly, tossing her head so that her hair fell perfectly back onto her shoulders. "He's not so bad. Kind of stuffy, but—"

"But the students who hang out in there?"

Lee had years of experience working with teenagers. Admittedly, they were more typically college-aged students scrambling for grants and internships from the Institute, but the emotions were all the same, under the surface. He skimmed the possibilities and took a guess. "The redheaded girl, Willow, can be rather possessive, can't she? I felt almost as though she didn't want me intruding on her territory."

The brunette's body language changed completely, and he knew he'd struck gold. He gave her a carefully paternal smile.

"It would help me a great deal if you could, perhaps, explain the situation for me. So that I don't blunder quite so badly the next time I need information." He paused, looking at his watch. "It's after noon already— if you haven't yet eaten, may I buy you lunch?"

Cordelia sized the man up, not too obviously, one part of her brain evaluating the potential for threat, the other noting to the dollar how much his outfit had cost.

Jacket, eh. Shirt is cotton, but quality. Slacks okay, nothing much. Nice shoes, though. Definitely Italian leather.

"Sorry, we're not supposed to leave campus." That was a lie, but Cordelia wasn't about to go off-campus anywhere with some guy she didn't know, even if he did dress okay. And killer eyes, the kind that look like they're made out of dark chocolate.

"Of course." He shrugged, one shoulder rising in a way that was coolly casual, like it didn't matter one way or another to him. "And I should know better. If any of my students had accepted such an invitation . . ."

"You're a teacher?"

She lost interest rapidly at that. There was absolutely no coolness factor in talking to a teacher, even if he was slightly cute.

"Ah, no. At least, not here. I've taught at the university level, but right now, I'm on sabbatical, working on a pet project of mine."

Okay, college professor was better.

He paused, giving her a long, considering look. "You grew up around here, didn't you? Perhaps you could help me . . ." He tilted his head, smiling at her. "As I said before, I fear I've fumbled badly, and your help would be a great aid."

Right. And I'm the Queen of Sheba. He wants something. Cordelia gave an inward shrug. *But he's easy on the eyes, and pretty much harmless . . . and if he tries anything, I've got some killer moves I picked up last summer.*

She smiled brightly at him, as much to wash away those memories as to accept his invitation, turning them both away from the library door. Her bag, still off-balance from their first encounter, swung out, hit the wall, and spilled open, scattering her belongings over the floor.

"Oh, darn it, I'm such a klutz. Hang on. No, that's

okay, I'll get everything." She knelt, tossing things back into the leather bag. When her hand closed on the compact, she opened it, just to make sure the mirror hadn't broken. His concerned face reflected from over her shoulder, and she closed the compact with a satisfied snap. It might be daylight, but a girl had to be careful about the company she kept. "I have some time now, if you want . . ."

"Now would be perfect, thank you. Is there a place we could sit and talk?"

The courtyard was bustling, some students hurrying to class, others taking advantage of the sunshine and a free period to lounge on benches or sit on the grass. Cordelia found them a free bench, made sure that Harmony and her flock of geese noticed this dish of an older guy paying attention to her, then sat down next to her companion, turning on the Chase charm.

"I have to admit, Willow probably had a reason for being stand-offish. We don't get too many outsiders using the high school library."

He gave her the barest hint of an answering smile. "No, I would think not. I merely was following up on a hobby of mine."

"A hobby . . . ?" Cordelia asked warily. Hobbies, in her experience, indicated losers who couldn't handle important things. Like shopping.

"Ah, yes. My work—I am a marine biologist—has given me an endless fascination with how much we don't know about the sea. There are a great many strange stories about the sea. Legends, myths, about the beings within it."

"Oh. You mean, like . . . supernatural beings." Well,

there went another potentially nice afternoon. What *was* it with this town, anyway?

He made a sort of embarrassed grimace. "Perhaps. Perhaps not. The sea is where we all come from, the mother of all life on this planet. Who are we to say that there isn't life still within its waters that we simply haven't encountered yet?"

Cordelia was becoming intrigued, despite herself. "You mean, like those plant-tube things they found on the floor of the ocean, the ones that live near heat vents? I read about them. Somewhere."

"Yes, exactly." He beamed at her, like she'd just won a prize. "But those are simple life-forms. What if something more advanced also swam in the depths? Or, perhaps, even closer to the surface?"

He leaned forward, his gaze suddenly boring into her. "Have you ever heard of the selkies? The seal people?"

Whoa. Ariel. Alarm bells suddenly clanging in her brain, Cordelia said warily, "Yes. Why?"

To her surprise, Dr. Lee's intense gaze dropped. Staring at the grass under their feet as though suddenly too embarrassed for words, he muttered, "It's . . . too unbelievable . . ."

For Sunnydale? That's so not possible! "What?" When he didn't answer, Cordelia persisted, "It's okay. Trust me, this town doesn't want to know about unbelievable. They're the masters of not-knowing."

And who would she tell? Not the losers back in the library, that was for sure. Unless, of course, he wanted to hunt Ariel, like that bounty hunter did with Oz? But who'd want to hurt a little kid like that? For her pelt? Ugh. Who'd wear a sealskin nowadays? Wasn't it on the endangered list, anyway? Or something like that. If her mother didn't own one, it had to be illegal *and* unfashionable.

"Ah . . . well." Dr. Lee glanced up at her again, all at once looking incredibly weary. "They're more than a legend, Ms. Chase. They're real."

"Uh-huh. And you know this because . . . ?"

"Because I married one."

CHAPTER 11

"**M**arried!" It came out as a startled squeak. "But she's just a—" *Oh, way to go, Chase. Give the whole thing away.* "I mean, a human and a seal?"

Lee played with the end of his tie, already clearly regretting his outburst, and Cordelia felt a frisson of panic. She needed to know what he was going to say. If this had anything to do with Ariel—if he wanted to hurt her—

You're going to do what? she wondered. *Stamp your foot, and demand that he unhand that seal? Be realistic. There's nothing you can do but stay out of this crazy guy's way. Remember? No more saving the world? Cordelia first, second, and last?*

On the other hand, information was power. And one needed that to get by in this town.

"I'm sorry," she said finally. "Please. Tell me?"

He let go of his tie, smoothed it back down, and

looked her straight in the eyes. "Maelen was a woman, Ms. Chase. Not human, but so very beautiful. Almost as lovely," he added bitterly, "as she was deceitful."

Oh. I know that tune. Boy, do I know that tune. The feeling of kinship she suddenly felt for the older man made her sympathy more real. "What happened?"

"We met on a beach one morning. Purely by accident. I was still a student, working on my graduate thesis. The sea, the sound of it, used to soothe me, calm my brain after a long night of research."

He frowned, looking out at the sunlit day, but obviously not seeing anything in the here-and-now.

"She was walking along the shoreline, her feet in the froth of the water. I fell for her at first sight, just like some boy in a song, and she, I thought, fell just as strongly for me."

"And?"

"I knew what she was, of course. As I said, my hobby was the study of mythology—even then, I knew more about selkies than most of the so-called scholars. But it didn't matter to me. And it didn't matter to her. I thought so, then. She gave up her seal-form, to live with me, to be my wife."

"And you didn't live happily ever after."

"Five years. And then she left me, abandoned me without a word, without a note, to return to the waters. Her vows meant nothing, our love meant nothing. She made a fool out of me. But I didn't care. I tried to follow her, but she was gone."

Dr. Lee stopped, turning to face Cordelia for the first time since he started his story. His face was absolutely without expression, but his eyes were full of pain. "No reason, no warning. Suddenly, my life was meaningless. And yet no one would believe me, thinking me maddened with grief until I learned to keep silent."

Then he looked up at her, as though half-expecting her to call out the loony police. "The ultimate betrayal—is that too fantastic a story for a young woman like you to comprehend?"

Cordelia forced a laugh. "Believe me, compared to what goes on in this neighborhood, that's nothing! And, well, as for the betrayal bit, I know *exactly* what you mean."

"Then you do understand." Dr. Lee leaned forward, not quite taking her hands. "My dear Ms. Chase, I know a selkie is being harbored in this town, by that young girl, Willow, who has a very kind heart, perhaps the others helping her as well. It isn't so surprising; selkies can be so very, very charming when it suits their mood. But a selkie isn't human, Ms. Chase. It doesn't think like us, it doesn't act like us. It can't. The destruction of a human life, of human lives . . . I haven't been able to learn if they're playing a cruel game with us, destroying us first with hope, then with despair, or whether they have some genuine, organized plot. But either way, I—I am determined to see that no one is ever taken in by one of those soulless creatures again."

Cordelia drew back in her seat. "I, uh, sure. That's very brave of you." She felt like she was leaning over the edge of a really high cliff, her balance all shaky. On the one hand, Ariel. Cute, quite defenseless. Not what you'd consider a major threat to a town that faced vampires and demons on a nightly basis. On the other hand, Dr. Lee really, really believed what he was saying. And everything he was saying was pretty believable. *I mean, look at Angel. Gorgeous face, and a vampire. Not all bad things are ugly on the outside.*

"I warn you, Ms. Chase, your friends are in great danger. They've been taken in by the selkie's charms. But it will not hesitate to do them harm if that suits its purpose."

Please. A broken heart doesn't mean all selkies are dangerous. Exaggeration—it's not just for kids. "Oh gee, look at the time." Cordy flashed her most charming smile. "I really do have to be going. Classes, you know?"

He didn't try to stop her. "Remember, Ms. Chase. As long as they harbor the selkie, as long as they are taken in by her charms, your friends are in danger."

She nodded. "Right. I'll keep that in mind."

What she really wanted to do was scrub the entire encounter out of her mind, the way one would scrape mud off the bottom of your shoe. But she couldn't. His face, all scrunched up in pain, kept alternating in her thoughts with Ariel's big brown eyes, all warm and trusting.

All right. She'd go to the library, warn Giles, and get out of there before any of the others could say anything. So everyone knew what everyone else was up to. Balanced scale, right? And whatever happened after that, well, it wasn't her problem.

It's not as if I care. Really. I'm just doing it to . . . to be fair.

CHAPTER 12

"**H**rrrm," Giles said. "Well."

"Hello?" Buffy asked. "Yes?"

"A moment, please," he replied, clearly irritated at being interrupted. Magnifying glass in hand, he was closely examining a strand of the clump of greenish hair Buffy had presented him with, ignoring the fact that by this late in the afternoon, it was beginning to stink like long-dead fish.

Of course, it wasn't all that much worse than what the library had stunk like that morning, Buffy thought. Giles had been out all day, meeting with that demonolo-whatever guy, so they hadn't been able to do anything until he got back but slog through classes and, in Buffy's case, deal with a surprise quiz that apparently hadn't been a surprise to anyone else in the class.

So unfair, she thought briefly. Even more so when Giles had corralled them after school to run some of the tests his friend had suggested. Willow the Junior Watcher might find all this stuff fascinating, but it was giving Buffy hives.

"Yes, this should work," Giles said almost to himself, reaching for a big glass bottle, filled with a weirdly glittery clear liquid.

"Well?" Buffy prodded impatiently. She bet this stuff was going to stink, too. Why did *everything* this week have to smell so bad? She was never going to get it out of her pores.

Behind them, Ariel had started whining softly, like an overtired kid, and the sound was really getting on her nerves. "Calm down," Buffy snapped over her shoulder, "we haven't forgotten you."

"Don't be mean to her!" Willow scolded, rushing to the selkie girl's side. "Poor Ariel isn't feeling well, are you?"

But Ariel refused to be comforted, moving here, there, not exactly pacing, just—moving. She definitely wasn't feeling well. Her once-sleek hair was dull, and her skin was papery and flushed. Even hours-long soaks in a tub weren't a good enough replacement for the ocean. Buffy wanted to feel sorry for her, but right now things that liked to munch on people *and* vampires were a higher priority.

And that's just the way Sunnydale works. Sorry.

Willow managed to coax Ariel back to a chair, one hand wiping a thin line of sweat off the selkie's forehead.

"She's got a fever!"

"I'll go get her some water," Xander said. "Dunk her head or something, maybe."

"Put salt in it!" Willow told him.

"Hang on, I'll go with you," Oz said. "See if we can't scrounge up a bucket or something."

"Cowards," Buffy said. "Running from a little smell?"

"Big smell," Oz corrected her, in his typical laconic fashion.

Xander nodded his head emphatically. "And just when you think it's gotten as bad as it could get, they do something that makes it worse."

"Oh, go on. Bunch of wimps," Willow said affectionately. Buffy wanted to join them as they escaped into the hallway, but anything Willow and Giles could stand, she could, too.

She thought.

"Based on our limited testing facilities," Giles said, oblivious to the banter around him, "I think it is safe to conclude that this is, indeed, hair."

Buffy sighed. "Well, gee, Giles, I never would have guessed. No, never mind. What *kind* of hair?"

He was dipping the ends of the strands into the clear liquid, which actually smelled sharply of spearmint. *Okay, slightly better smell. But only slightly.* "Well?"

Giles stretched the hair out on a sheet of white paper, watching for some kind of reaction. "Wait a moment . . ." The paper turned a watery blue-green color, then darkened into a gross brown. He glanced up, pushing his glasses absently back up on his nose.

"The pH balance of the strands, plus their reaction when exposed to—" he rattled off something many-syllabled that Buffy guessed had to be some, well, chemagical substance related to the sea "—would confirm that we are definitely dealing with a being that spends the majority of its lifespan in the ocean. Not that this was much in doubt, by now, but it is always good to have confirmation of these things.

"However, none of our research has turned up any creature, supernatural or otherwise, that will come out of the water to feed in such a frenzy—and off humans and vampires alike. Especially as food seems to be a lesser priority, since not much of the bodies was consumed."

"That we know of," Buffy said. "Maybe they like to drag their food off somewhere else to eat it, like crocodiles. Or maybe they weren't real hungry when they got here. If they're being drawn to the Hellmouth, like you said, then I bet they've worked up an appetite by now."

"True." He paused. "It would help cut down our research considerably if we knew if it was one creature, or many."

"One would be better, right?" Willow asked hesitantly.

Buffy and Giles looked at each other, then Giles shook his head. "Ordinarily, having to deal with one such creature would be best, yes. However, the thought of a single creature that would cause this much damage and fear among the vampire population . . ."

"Oh." Willow curled her arm protectively around Ariel and swallowed hard.

It was ironic, Angel thought, that his weakness—his vampire nature—was so often the one source of strength he could offer Buffy. What made their personal relationship impossible, strengthened their working relationship. Slayer and vampire, fighting the forces of darkness, side by side . . .

Or, in this case, apart. He had walked her home that morning, watching until she had gotten inside the safety of the house, then gone to catch some downtime himself. But all he could think about were those vampires, trapped in the sewer and torn apart by some creature or creatures that didn't seem to have any trouble taking them down.

What could have done that? And how?

And so, the moment the early dusk had fallen, he had begun patrolling, keeping his body busy in the faint hope that his mind would slow down.

Buffy had brought the hair they'd found to Giles, to see what the Watcher might have to say, and was probably still with him, trying to figure out what it was they were facing. It was better that way. Better he not have to go into the library. Better he not have to see the rest of the Slayerettes, Giles . . .

"Don't go there," he told himself sternly, using Buffy's favorite phrase of the moment. He was making a career out of Not Going There. It was a more active pastime than brooding, but nowhere near as poetic.

It hurt more, too. Everything seemed to hurt, these days. Except when he was with Buffy.

Okay, enough of that. Keep your mind on the job at hand. If anyone could figure it out, it would be Giles. Angel, unlike the Slayerettes, never underestimated the intelligence that fueled the Watcher, nor the resources he had available to him.

"Hey!"

The startled cry had him moving forward without conscious thought, ready to break up any human/vampire clinch he encountered. Swinging over a high backyard fence, Angel landed on his feet, crouching slightly as he prepared to do battle.

But what greeted him wasn't the usual ridged face

and fanged mouth of his demonic relations. Instead, the human male was caught unprepared in his own yard, gripped in a headlock by a slender, sexless creature, its skin glowing a faint silvery-green, long green hair growing from the crest of its bullet-shaped head. Round, black eyes, set slightly to the sides of its face, blinked once at him, and the pale mouth opened to show a double row of small, sharp teeth.

It was like falling into the mouth of a shark.

Like staring into the eyes of a viper.

And Angel, for all that he had died over two hundred years before, felt a sudden shake of fear.

This was *malice*.

The creature bent down and tore a chunk out of the human's neck, its dead eyes never leaving Angel's. It chewed, and the vampire felt his gorge rise as he realized that the man was still alive, moaning in disbelieving pain.

Angel backed up one step, moving cautiously, and felt hard, scaled hands come down on his shoulders from behind him.

Xander threw up his hands in an exaggerated shrug. "Well, how was I supposed to know that bucket was part of the sophomore art display?"

"The fact that it was in a display case?" Oz suggested mildly. "Or maybe—Hey, Cordelia," he added, side-stepping just in time to avoid a collision.

She pulled away, smoothing back her hair and trying to look nonchalant. But the way her glance kept flicking down the hall, toward the library, gave away her purpose.

"Don't you two have homes to go to?" she asked. "I

mean, I know Xander doesn't. But there must be someone who wants to see you, Oz."

"Oh look," Xander promptly retorted, pretending to be speaking only to Oz, "it's Cordelia. Isn't she a—"

"Whoa." Oz held up his hands. "Time out. Play nice."

"I wasn't—"

"I didn't—"

"Cordelia," Oz cut in hastily, "what's bothering you? Besides Xander."

She bit her lip, turning so that Xander was excluded from their conversation as much as she could manage. "Whatever it is you're doing, which I don't want to know, by the way, is getting some interest you probably don't want."

"Who? Dr. Lee?" Xander forgot to be annoyed. "We know. We took care of him."

"I know. I mean, you didn't. Take care of him. He's pretty sure you're hiding something. Oz, he knows about Ariel! I don't know how, but he does—"

"She probably told him," Xander muttered.

"I did not!" she snapped, then turned back to Oz. "He figured it out himself. That's a guy who's not as wrapped as he should be. He thinks all selkies are the worst kind of monster, which proves that he hasn't been in *this* town very long."

Xander groaned. "Great, just great. Did you ever stop to think that Lee was probably using you to see how much we really did know, Miss Subtle?"

"Well, catch *me* warning you about anything again!" Cordy exploded. "You deal with it on your own, then. Or just let Buffy handle it for you. As always."

Cordelia stalked off before Xander could come up with a coherent comeback.

X

"No time, Xander," Oz warned, his gaze flicking down the hallway, where Dr. Lee was coming around the corner.

Xander groaned. "Great. Okay, follow me, and remember—when in doubt, act like an idiot."

Pasting a false grin on his face, Xander rushed up to greet Dr. Lee. "Hi! I didn't get a chance to talk to you before, and I really, really wanted to."

As Dr. Lee tried to move past Xander, Oz moved in to block his path. "That's right! We don't often get a chance to ask questions of someone so important, who's actually been out there and done stuff."

It was practically a speech for Oz, and Xander was impressed, despite himself. Who knew the other guy had so many words in him? All at one time, too?

Dr. Lee, on the other hand, didn't seem to be impressed. "I'm sorry, but I'm—"

"That's right," Xander agreed. "D'you know, just the other day I was saying to Oz, that's this guy here, 'Oz, I really need to learn more about fish.'"

"I really am in a bit of a hurry—"

"No prob," Xander continued, interrupting the scientist gleefully. "It's just that everyone tells us we don't ask enough questions. You know, further our education and all that. So," he continued with desperate cheerfulness, "what *do* you think dolphins are really saying?"

"Eeeuww," said a sudden disgusted voice. "What *are* you doing in here?"

Buffy didn't bother glancing up: Cordy. "New perfume. 'Eau de Seaweed.'"

"Amusing. Un."

Giles looked over his glasses at her. "Cordelia? Is there something I can do for you?"

Cordy hesitated, looking almost nervous. "I . . . Dr. Lee? The guy who was in here before?"

Buffy straightened. *Oh great, I knew he was going to cause trouble.* "What about him?"

"He wanted to have lunch with me." She tossed her head so that her hair fell over one shoulder perfectly. "Not so surprising, I mean, older man, younger woman, you know . . ."

Giles frowned ever so slightly. "Cordelia, please. We're rather busy here."

"He's hunting seal-people," she burst out. "I know, anywhere else that would be like so crazed. But crazy's kind of a way of life around here, right?" Cordelia took a deep breath, seeing she had their undivided attention.

"He told me he was married to one, and that she abandoned him and went back to the sea." She stopped, blinking. "Is that, like, possible? I mean, a seal and—"

"Yes, yes," Giles said, his expression changing from irritation to comprehension. "In the folklore, at any rate."

"An abandoned husband," Buffy murmured. "Out to get revenge. Ha, I bet I'm right! He can't hate her, he still kinda loves her, so he's going to get her family instead. Ariel—"

"That's right!" Cordy cut in. "Giles, he knows about Ariel. I didn't tell him a thing, I swear it, but somehow he knew that Willow'd been hiding her. He thinks she's some kind of danger, which makes him really pitiful, being scared of a little kid—"

"He won't get anywhere near her," Buffy said shortly. "We'll stop him."

For a second, she was surprised at her own fierceness. But then she realized, *All right, so I don't feel comfortable about her. Built-in Slayer stuff, I can't do anything about that.*

But I am so not going to let some idiot of a human murder her, either!

After Cordelia left, any responsibility discharged and forgotten, Xander and Oz came back, having finally given up on their bucket quest, but pleased to relay their successful harassment and scaring off of Dr. Lee.

"For now, anyway," Giles said. "But if he is as obsessed as Cordelia indicated—"

"He's not going to give up," Buffy finished for him. "Not unless we make him."

"Maybe not even then," Oz said.

"He's such a comfort, isn't he?" Xander asked the room in general.

Oz shrugged and went to join his girlfriend, who was sitting on the stairs, trying to calm the selkie down.

"Ariel, *ciunas*," she said soothingly, trying to pass a dampened cloth over the little girl's still-flushed skin. "Ariel!"

The selkie dodged her outstretched hand, continuing to move restlessly, whining.

"Ariel, please!" Willow held out both arms this time, trying to corral the selkie without making it look as though she was trying to catch her. "Guys, help me out here!"

"*Casog!*" Ariel insisted, eyes so wide Willow could see the white rimming the dark irises. "*Cota!*"

"That means 'coat,' doesn't it?" she asked in despair.

"What? Oh, yes," Giles said from where he and Buffy were trying to put together a strategy to deal with Lee.

"Coat. Right. Ariel, I know no one's working on cleaning it right this very second. But we haven't forgotten, honest!" As Ariel ducked under Xander's arm, and evaded Oz's grab, Willow called to Giles, "She's getting hysterical! You've got to say something to calm her!"

"Ariel, you have not been forgotten . . . ah . . . *dearmad no,* which is highly ungrammatical but should get the point across. Yes, that's right, Ariel. *Dearmad no,* aren't forgetting. But if we don't take care of this other difficulty first, you may not have a family to return to. And you probably aren't getting a word of this, but frankly, I am all out of Gaelic! So sit down, and do shut up!"

"Gee, Giles," Buffy said, "tsk. Losing your cool in front of students. Bad example."

"Funny, Buffy. Really. Now—what is it?"

Buffy shook her head, feeling every nerve suddenly go on alert. "Not sure . . . Angel!"

The vampire staggered in, his usual grace completely gone. Although the cuts and welts on his skin didn't appear to be too bad, there was an overall sense of exhaustion about him that made the three nearest humans start forward to catch him before he collapsed.

"What happened?" Buffy demanded as they lowered him into a chair.

"I didn't know anything could whomp on a vampire like that," Willow said, half in awe, from her location on the stairs. "Except you, of course, Buffy."

"They can't, as a general rule," Giles said. "Being undead limits the kind of damage that can be inflicted on a vampire. Short of dusting one—"

"Their claws, some kind of poison. Hard to move . . ." Angel winced as Buffy helped him take off his long coat, revealing a long tear down the front of his shirt, as though he had been scored by sharp, talonlike claws.

Ariel took one look and hid her face under Oz's arm.

"Neurotoxin. Some sea creatures use it to stun their prey. Fascinating, that it works on demons . . ."

"Giles, research another time!" Buffy demanded.

The Watcher, however, was clearly focused on the moment. "These were the creatures that attacked the vampires earlier? And the humans on the beach?"

Angel nodded his head weakly. "Either that, or we've got way too much company in town."

"What did they look like?" Giles asked, while, behind him, Willow opened the *Big Book of Marine Demons*.

"Humanish. Green, scaled. Long hair, like Buffy found."

"Told you it was hair," Buffy grumbled.

"And teeth," Angel continued, shaking off the remaining effects of the toxin. "Too many teeth for the size of their mouths. They fight in a pack, like wolves. One of them distracted me, the others closed in from behind. Hit me. They've got hard hands, fins, something, I don't know. Took me out with one swipe. I came to, and they were all around me, like I was dinner . . ."

"Well, there's a new sensation for a demon," Giles murmured, not without some satisfaction.

Angel acknowledged the hit, but kept talking. "The one I surprised, it was . . . it was eating a human. Just taking chunks out of him, still screaming. When he died, it lost interest. They only like their food alive."

"But then why attack vampires?" Buffy wondered.

"Not for food," Giles said. "At least, not after the

first attack, I should suppose. They must not be able to tell the difference without actual physical contact."

"You mean . . . taste?" Willow asked in a small voice.

Angel nodded his agreement. "They didn't seem to know what I was, at least until after they dropped me. Then they kicked me around some, while I couldn't move, then just left me there."

"Merrows," Giles said in sudden realization. "Blast it, of course! We were so busy looking for something, someone, who would normally stay in the shallows or come out of the water, yes, *and* feed on vampires—We were totally misdirected!"

"Merrows," Buffy said flatly, in her "someone had better explain it all to me *now*" voice.

"Unpleasant cousins to the traditional mermaid—who isn't such a charming being herself, come to think of it—"

Buffy cut off a scholarly tangent at the source. "Giles? Merrows?"

"Right. They are humanoid, that is, biped rather than with bodies tapering to a tail—and they will catch and eat any humans they can drag off ships."

"Geez. So much for 'See the charming Pacific Coast by cruise ship!' " Xander said. "But what's making them come in to land—whoa. The oil spill."

"Exactly." Giles removed his glasses and gestured with them. "The oil spill. Just as it interfered with other natural sea creatures, it must have interfered with the merrows as well. Evolution in response to environmental changes . . ." He drifted off in thought, his eyes looking somewhere else, the way they did when he got caught up in a really neat new idea.

"Can we talk Greenpeace later?" Buffy asked. "So we've got another big bad evil in town. Not a problem. I ask them politely to leave, and when they don't, I kick their nonexistent tails."

"It won't be that easy," Angel said, straightening up with an effort. "Giles, if you're right, and the merrows are changing their feeding grounds, the vampires in this area aren't going to just sit back and let it happen. And if they start fighting . . ."

"Oh dear."

"What?" Buffy looked between the two of them. "Merrows, bad. I think we got that, Giles." Her eyes narrowed as she caught the gist of what they were thinking. "Are you saying we're going to have gang warfare breaking out among the undead and the unhuman?"

Angel nodded. "The Hellmouth as the prize. And humans caught in the crossfire."

"Oh, great," Xander said. "Sunnydale's own version of the Crips and Bloods."

"Alpha predators." Oz had been quiet for so long, they'd almost forgotten he was there. Ariel still huddled under his arm, occasionally sneaking a peek at the long, jagged rip down Angel's shirt, then hiding again.

"Yes, I suspect you're right," Giles said.

"Explain that for the rest of us, okay?" Buffy demanded.

"It's a food chain thing," Willow said. "You've got plants; then herbivores, the prey animals; then little predators that feed on the prey; then bigger predators that feed on the little predators. And they all live happily ever after—although not very happily for the ones who always get eaten," she added with a frown. "Happily, I mean, only if the chain isn't broken."

"But the getting-eaten side's being disrupted by the oil spill," Xander said. "Hence, merrows in the water supply."

Willow nodded. "Vampires are the alpha predators in Sunnydale. They're tougher than just about anything else, they're more efficient hunters, and they're a lot stronger. Merrows come in, they're not top dog anymore. There's not room enough for both of them in this food chain."

"There's not room for either one of them," Buffy said. "Not while I'm on the job."

"Yes. Well," Giles said. "I would suggest that we focus our attention on the merrows, for now. I hate to say this, but right now, vampires do seem to be the lesser of two evils."

Xander shook his head. "And we really, really hate hearing you say it, Giles."

It was false dawn, when the sky lightens just enough to make some early-rising birds think it's time to start singing. But night still holds court, and vampires walk freely.

And on this night, there was a method to their walking.

"Seen anything?" a stalking vampire hissed to another. He moved with the powerful forward surge of the football player he had been in life. Anger was evident in every ragged line. He'd seen what these creatures could do, and he wanted a piece of them in return. Nobody took his prey. *Nobody!*

The second vampire, a gaunt-faced woman, gave him a snarl of disgust. "Nothing. Not even prey. You?"

The first vampire clenched his fists. "Nothing. Yet."

Neither of them was happy so close to the other: None of them were, not without a Master to follow. But by unvoiced agreement, the vampires of Sunnydale were playing well together. For tonight. For as long as this state of siege lasted.

Then the wind changed slightly and brought them something.

"Salt," the first said succinctly, and lunged.

The next followed a second later, catching the lone merrow, the foolish scout, between them. It snarled and clawed at them, biting at their flesh, but other vampires came rushing, pulled by the scent of ocean and blood. Not human blood, not something worth drinking, but they were after more this time.

There were snarls, screams, then the wet, soft sound of flesh being torn . . .

The vampires straightened, spitting to clear their mouths of the taste of that too-salty, too-alien blood, some of them staggering from the poisonous residue left by the creature's claws. The body of the merrow lay strewn in ragged pieces over the ground.

Poachers could not be—would not be—tolerated.

The war had begun.

CHAPTER 13

He didn't know what he was doing back here. Returning to the scene of the crime only worked in detective novels, where the brilliant sleuth would discern from a piece of trampled carpeting that the killer was forty-three, five feet ten inches tall, and had a predilection for bologna sandwiches.

Lee sat down heavily on the low seawall and stared out into the waters. He had loved the ocean, once. He had gone into his career wanting nothing more than to know everything he could about the life that swam within its waters. To eke out every bit of mystery it hid, and make it his own.

He had been after science. What he had discovered was legend.

Legend, and pain.

"I miss you, Maelen," he said softly, for no one to hear. "Why did you make me fall in love with you?

Was it only a game? Did it please you to see me that way? Did it please you to destroy me?"

He didn't expect an answer. He had never gotten one before, not in eleven long and solitary years. He had encountered four selkies after Maelen left him. Three died before he could question them, and one had spat in his face before escaping, disappearing off the side of the small research boat the Institute had loaned him.

The cleanup was still going on out there, though, as the media kept insisting cheerfully, "We were lucky this time." Not as bad as it might have been. But reports would still be coming in via e-mail and fax from up and down the coast—E.L.F. volunteers and professionals alike, doing their bit to correct the damage done. Ritchie would be back at the lab, compiling the reports, highlighting information Lee would need to know to estimate the true extent of that damage. He should be back there, organizing, doing the job the Institute had hired him to do.

But on this stretch of beach, its sand showing only the normal debris of the ocean, it was easy to sit and try to forget.

The waves wash everything clean. Everything, except the memory. And the pain.

Reaching under his jacket, Lee removed the pistol, letting its weight lie heavy and comforting in his palm. It was useless. It solved nothing. But sometimes merely knowing it was there gave him some feeling of control over the world.

Xander stopped short, nearly sliding on sandy rocks. There he was, Dr. Lee, sitting there like—

Whoa! Like a man with a gun.

"Dr. Lee!"

Oh yeah, right, get his attention. Way to go.

Lee turned sharply. To Xander's relief, he put the gun away, not rushing the movement, saying without words, see, not a threat. "Hello. We've . . . met?"

"Xander. Xander Harris. We met at the high school?"

"Ah, yes. You were trying to keep me out of the library."

Xander almost choked on his next words. *Busted,* he thought. *Guess that old question-and-divert thing doesn't work as well as it used to in math class.* "Um, well— okay, yeah. We were." He paused. "But if you knew . . ."

Lee shook his head, turning to look back at the ocean. "You're hiding something from me. But I can't force you to believe me, force you to trust me. I can only pray that no harm comes to anyone while you make up your mind."

Xander had been prepared for some fire-and-brimstone preacher type. Not this sad, hollow-eyed old guy. Suddenly, he wanted Willow there with him. Will would know what to say, to do. Him? He was the King of Bad Speaking, the sure person to say the wrong thing at the wrong time. And this felt about as much as wrong place, wrong time as anything ever had.

So he just clenched his teeth and said nothing.

I knew it was a bad idea. "Come on, Xander," Buffy said. "Just see where he goes, what he does. And, you know, keep him out of trouble." *Yeah, right.*

But Oz had band practice, and Willow was keeping tabs on Ariel, and Buffy and Giles were going over her dreams with a fine-tooth comb, trying to get everything they could out of them. So that left him.

See where he goes, what he does. Only, the guy

didn't seem like he was going anywhere, much less into trouble.

The waves crested and broke, and finally Lee sighed, shaking his head. "You know something, all of you. I can see it in your eyes. You know the danger you're in—"

"But you don't."

The moment the words were out of his mouth, Xander could have kicked himself. *Oh, brilliant. Why not just give him the secret handshake and invite him into the club?*

"I assure you, I'm quite aware—"

"No, you're not." Might as well cram both feet in there, while he was at it. This guy was supposed to be so brilliant, let him chew on reality for a bit. Giles could yell at him later. "Matter of fact, you don't have a clue."

Lee sprang to his feet, his face contorted with anger. "How dare you! They gnaw at the heart of humanity, destroying bonds of family and—"

"Okay, if you start on the whole Family Values thing, I'm out of here," Xander said in disgust, turning away. "I'm sure you're—" He broke off, looking down the beach. "Uh-oh."

"What?"

But Xander had already set off at a run, the sand kicking up from underneath his sneakers. Behind him, Lee followed at a more cautious pace as he reached the . . . object.

What it was, was an arm. A human arm. Unattached to anything resembling a human body.

"Oh, God," Lee said softly.

Xander suspected he was more than a little green

around the gills himself, but held himself together enough to look for more body parts.

"Ugh."

He'd just found the rest of the upper torso, half-hidden under a clump of seaweed-entangled driftwood. A man's torso and head. The man's face was still scrunched up in fear and horror, eyes closed as though denying whatever it was that had come after him.

"No," Xander said when Lee would have come closer. "I really don't think you want to see this." *Hey,* his mind gibbered, I *don't want to see this.*

Wait a minute . . . Xander tugged at the body, twisting the still-attached arm so that the patch on the jacketed arm was revealed.

It was a square patch, dark blue, with a stylized wave in sea-green, and three letters: E.L.F.

"Oh, God," Willow said. "Oh, God."

Buffy dumped her into a chair before she could pass out.

"Oh, God," she said again.

Xander had used Dr. Lee's minicorder to make notes on the scene, then booked it back to the library, leaving Dr. Lee to call the police and make a report. The less Xander's name was associated with gruesome deaths and weird happenings, the better he liked it. Besides, as Xander had reasonably pointed out, Lee had a reason to be on the beach, while he was supposed to be in class.

"Oh, God," Willow said again.

"Breathe, Willow," Giles urged her.

"Right. Breathing. Oh, poor Sean. He was our team leader, it was his job to go over the site afterward and make sure everything looked okay, that we hadn't missed any spots or left any tools. He must have gone back and . . ." She swallowed, her control visibly slamming down on her emotions. Buffy hated that. You always knew where you stood with Willow, everything on the surface and honest. She shouldn't have to be stoic about a friend dying.

Yeah, but sometimes stoic hurts less. We're getting way too much practice at this.

Besides, right now, Willow was the only person who could give them the information they needed. Voice carefully businesslike, Buffy asked, "So he would have had a reason to be there, exactly where you guys were working?"

Willow nodded.

"And there's no reason for him to go there at night, if he was checking on your work?"

Willow shook her head.

"Definitely diurnal, or at least, not restricted to nocturnal activities," Giles said thoughtfully.

"Which means that whatever it is, it's still hanging around," Xander said with a shudder. "It could have been just lurking there in the water while I was there. Okay, I vote for breaking out the heavy artillery now, and not waiting until we actually have it in our sights, okay?"

Buffy was pretty much in agreement with Xander. The fact that part of the body had been chewed off confirmed—like she needed it!—that they were dealing with people-eaters. Buffy didn't have warm-and-fuzzies for things that ate people.

"And what did Lee have to say about all this?" she asked.

Xander shrugged. "Not much. Muttering stuff about the dangers of the sea. He's pretty much fixated on that whole selkie thing. Whatever his ex did to him, it must have been pretty bad."

"Broken hearts are ugly things," Buffy said with a little more force than she'd intended. "They can make you more than a little crazy."

"Well, Lee's on that road, and gaining speed." Xander stopped. "Where is Ariel, anyway?"

"Sleeping in my office," Giles said. "I managed to find a small tub in the hardware store, and we filled it with warm water. An infusion of salt crystals, some towels to line the bottom, and she appeared to be quite at home."

"She's getting awfully weak, though," Willow said. "Even with the salt water. I tried using the lotion Cordelia recommended, but—"

Xander's eyebrows shot up. "Cordelia?"

Buffy nodded. "Weird. She came by, about an hour after you left, with a whole bunch of stuff for Ariel. Toys, and the lotion."

"She wants to help," Willow said. "She just doesn't want to *help* help. I mean . . ."

"We know what you mean, Will," Buffy assured her.

"Oh. Well. Spells. We should be working, Giles, shouldn't we? Ariel can't stay in that tub forever!"

"Do what you can, okay?" Buffy said, reaching for her jacket.

"And where will you be?" Giles asked in his Watcher-must-know voice. Buffy grinned at him, so relieved to hear that tone directed at her again she didn't even bristle at having to check in. "Gonna go fishing," she said.

CHAPTER 14

"**W**ould anyone mind terribly if I went and hid behind something?"

"Thank you for the vote of confidence, Xander," Giles said over his shoulder. He was using a strip of dried salmon jerky to convince Ariel to sit still on the worktable, her soiled sealskin around her shoulders the way it had been when Willow had first found her.

"No problem," Xander said cheerfully.

After Buffy had left to find Angel, they had moved operations to the chemistry lab, in the hopes that Dr. Lee wouldn't think to hunt for them there, if he came back. Besides, while Willow was pretty sure she had the right spell, and the right spell components, any further mishaps here could be explained away as legitimate experiments if the results lingered until Monday. The spate of particularly bad smells in the library was starting to raise more questions than usual.

Plus, Giles was worried about his books. It was difficult to get the smell of iron sulfide out of parchment.

"Well, here goes . . . something," Willow muttered, stepping up to the table.

Her tee shirt was untucked from the waistband of her skirt, and she was barefoot. Next to her, Giles was also barefoot, his jacket off and his shirt undone. This part should have been skyclad, according to the spell book, completely naked, but Giles had firmly drawn the line at that. Unfastening everything seemed the best compromise.

Oz and Xander backed away to the far wall, unwilling to leave, but not wanting to be in the potential line of fire. Willow glanced once at Giles, then raised her hands, palms up, and chanted:

"In your truest form I conjure you."

One palm tipped, scattering a handful of colored salts onto the top of Ariel's head. The selkie tried to look up, to see what it was, but Giles's hand cupped her chin, keeping her still.

"In your truest form I cleanse you."

The other palm tipped, and a shower of glimmering dust fell, sparkling in the fluorescent lights and catching in Ariel's hair and eyelashes.

"In your truest form I release you."

Willow brought both hands together, then down slowly, smoothing the spell elements into Ariel's hair, and down into the skin, pressing firmly. Then she closed her eyes, concentrating on the rest of the spell, her lips moving silently as she traced the remaining steps of the modified changeling spell.

Ariel whined deep in her throat, but remained still under Giles's hand. The skin twitched slightly under

Willow's hand, a hazy glow forming in her palm, and drifting out to cover Ariel's shoulders, gathering over the surface of the sealskin.

"It's working . . ." Oz said in a whisper. Xander nodded, his nose wrinkling slightly as some of the spell dust reached them on a current from the school's ventilation system.

"Aegir, look upon your child with favor.

"Aegir, look upon your child with love.

"Release the bonds of human making.

"Release her to—"

"Haaa-chooo!"

Willow squeaked, Oz started, and Ariel leaped forward off the table, directly into Giles's arms. The glow burst like a soap bubble, and Watcher and selkie both fell over backward, landing on the tile floor with a loud and painful-sounding crash.

Xander, his hand covering his offended nose, blushed a deep, unattractive red. "Sorry."

"Xander!" Willow snapped, whirling toward him, her hands still coated with the faint shimmer of magickal residue. "We almost had it! Next time, I swear . . ."

"Willow, enough," Giles said from the floor. "At least we know that we're on the right track. Ariel?" he added, struggling back to his feet. "Are you all right? Uh . . . *follain?"*

The selkie, huddled on the ground, was sniffing anxiously at her skin. She turned large, pitiful eyes up at the Watcher, and said something in Gaelic that Willow guessed could only be, "It didn't work."

"Almost, child. Almost. Next time," Giles continued, turning to Willow, "we really must consider using sea salt, not rock salt."

Willow sighed. "Yeah. We both missed that one. I guess the health food store would—"

"Giles!"

Oz's call was cut off as he was hurled to the floor. The thing attacking him was almost twice his height, but the same mass; slender and wiry, shaped sort of like an eel, all sinew and streamlined muscle. But it didn't move so well, tumbling to the floor with the human, unable for a second to untangle itself. It paused long enough for a quick sniff, thin lips drawn back in a sneer, then scrambled over the boy, heading straight for Xander. Behind the first intruder, more forms crowded in the doorway.

Awkward movements, Giles noted, even as his body went into adrenaline overdrive. *Despite their strength and viciousness, they're not used to being on completely dry land. Right now, that's to our advantage. Perhaps our* only *advantage.*

Ariel! The selkie was the weakest of them all. If they were truly pack animals, they would go for the easiest kill first . . .

"Willow! Protect Ariel!"

The witch hastily pushed the terrified girl behind her, and sketched ritual gestures in the air. Magic sparkled from her fingers, enhanced by the spell ingredients still on her skin. Bright blue lines of protection encircled the two girls, moving with them as they backed out of the way. A simple distraction spell, Giles recognized, and not one that would hold up under direct attack, but it should keep them unnoticed. He hoped.

Meanwhile, Xander was doing remarkably well against the merrows who had tried to corner him against a lab table, snatching up a stool and breaking it over a green head. The merrow crumpled, and Giles thought, *Good lad.* His endless lectures on using whatever was to hand had taken root in at least one of his students. The Watcher-trained brain that never shut down noted that the stool had broken nicely into stake-sized pieces, as well.

Three of the creatures were trying to get Xander, and one was poking at Oz—

And that leaves one for me.

"Wonderful," Giles said.

Bring the fight to the enemy. Grabbing a handful of the spell components, he moved forward into the fray.

"On the count of three," Buffy murmured to Angel as they watched the solitary vampire pass in front of them.

"One . . ."

Angel leaped onto the vampire's back, taking him down, face first onto the sidewalk.

"Three," Buffy said, getting up and walking to where the two demons struggled. "Want some help?" she asked sweetly.

"No. I got it."

Angel finally managed to subdue his fiercely squirming target, holding him still on the ground. Her un-boyfriend, Buffy saw, had vamped out during the struggle, and two ridged expressions glared at each other until the pinned demon looked away.

"What you want, Slayer-toy?" he asked, his voice a rumbling growl. "Stake me, or let me go. I don't have time to chat tonight."

"Gee, I'm hurt. Now, what's so different about tonight?"

But that was apparently all the demon planned to share with them.

Angel shifted a little, adjusting his grip for long-term comfort, and noticed something on the shirt of his captive.

"Buffy. Look."

The Slayer leaned over, careful to keep herself just out of reach, should Angel's grip slip, and studied the dark green splotch Angel was indicating.

"Ooo, someone's been playing rough. Merrow blood's tough to get out, too."

The demon hissed, showing his fangs, but his eyes were suddenly sharply alert. "Merrows. Is that what they're called?"

Slayer and vampire exchanged a quick glance, then Buffy shrugged. *Might as well tell him what we know. Weird though it seems, we're fighting on the same team. Too bad Spike's not in town, him at least I could sort of figure out . . .*

"Merrows, yeah. Deep-sea flesh eaters. Horning in on your territory a little, huh? That's gotta sting. Not to mention the fact that they obviously don't think you're all too scary."

The demon lost it at that.

"We will drain their undrinkable blood till it flows back to the sea! Then we will throw their shredded bodies in as well! This town is ours!"

Buffy rolled her eyes and sighed dramatically. "Gee, what were you in life, a B-movie actor? What, you're going to fight it out until there's only one side left standing? Oh yeah, that's real practical. Typical demon thought process: if it moves, attack."

"Pot, kettle," Angel said, *sotto voce*.

"I heard that."

"I think he's told us everything he knows," Angel went on, hiding a faint smile at her aggrieved tone.

"I think you're right." Only Angel's hyper reflexes kept him from tumbling forward as the body he was restraining turned to dust.

"Sorry, my bad." She frowned. "You think he was serious? About the whole blood bath thing?"

"Yes. Demons tend to be short-tempered about being crowded."

"I've noted that, yeah. Pity I can't just let them wipe each other out. But they aren't going to stop with each other, are they?"

"I doubt it. And if the merrows win—"

"Then we've got people-eaters who aren't stopped by sunlight. Right. Come on. Giles and Willow were going to give the spell another shot, so they'll still be in the library. I want their brains in on this. We're going to stop it before it becomes a full-fledged turf war. Somehow."

Xander was panting and sweaty, flailing about at the merrows with whatever came to hand, but he wasn't scared. All right, not really grossed-out scared.

I've seen better special effects on the late night Monster Movie. He slapped a merrow across the face, hard, with one of the stool legs.

Out of the corner of his eye, Xander saw Oz getting to his knees, then diving for the merrow guarding him, toppling it to the floor. Willow was nowhere to be seen, neither was Ariel. *Maybe they got away.*

On the other side of the room, Giles dodged one merrow, ducking under its reach, then brought his hand down hard on another merrow's back. Dust rose, Giles's mouth moved in some kind of silent chant, and sparks danced along the creature's scales. It screamed, then fell to the ground, writhing in pain.

Supernatural creatures none, magic-using Watcher, one. Yay us.

"Hey!"

Cordelia barreled into the room, stopped short, and started rooting in her bag. *What's she doing here?* Xander wondered wildly. *What, does she just lurk until I'm in trouble, so she can see me get killed?* After a second that seemed like a lifetime to him, she snatched out a small cylinder and aimed it at the merrow nearest her.

"Eat spray, fishface!" she said, and hit the button, aiming a steady stream of Mace into its face.

The creature fell back, clawed hands scrabbling at its eyes. A high-pitched keening filled the air, and Oz almost fell again, hands over his ears as it hit registers only he of all the humans could hear.

The merrows still standing turned as one to stare at Cordelia, who backed up against the doorframe, unsure which one to spray next. Whatever she did, it would leave six to attack.

"Help?"

A faint *"eeep"* came from Willow's corner of the room, and the merrows turned with one accord, the distraction spell broken.

Giles rubbed his hands together, hoping for more of the spell dust. But there was nothing left.

"Damn," he muttered. Then Xander's shout made him lift his hand just in time to see one of the chair legs coming his way. He grabbed it, ignoring the splinters digging into his palm, and swung for the nearest green head.

Seven against four. Under normal circumstances, the humans wouldn't have stood a chance.

Since when, Giles thought, *have circumstances in Sunnydale ever remotely been normal?*

Taking advantage of the merrows' awkwardness, Oz rolled along the floor, playing bowling ball to the merrows' pins. He knocked two over, taking them out of the fray for a few essential seconds, while the others prepared to charge again.

"Willow!" Cordelia waved wildly at her, then at the open closet door: a possible hiding spot for Ariel. She sprang back with a startled "Ewww!" as a merrow and Xander fell at her feet, scrabbling wildly.

The merrow opened its mouth, preparing to deliver a nasty bite to Xander's forearm—but instead got a Ferragamo pump in its mouth.

"Ow! And those were new shoes, too!"

Xander brought the chair leg he was still clutching up into the merrow's rib cage, forcing it in with the strength of desperation. The scaled body froze, oozing green blood from the jagged wound, then slumped forward, knocking Xander back down to the ground.

"Guess I hit something he needed. Cordy! Behind you!"

Oz tackled that one, bringing it back down to the floor, and Giles stepped in to finish the kill with one quick, efficient blow with an intact chair. The remaining four creatures took one look at the changed odds and made a break for the door.

"No." Giles stopped Oz when he would have followed. "Let them go. They're deep-sea creatures: In the dark, their eyesight is better. They'd have the advantage again."

"No problem," Oz said, and sank to the floor beside Willow and Ariel, grinning and panting.

"Guys!"

Buffy skidded into the library, stopping when she saw that the room was empty.

"Guys?"

She took a tentative sniff of the air.

"No ickiness in the air. So . . . no spells? No gang."

She looked around again, half expecting them to be hiding somewhere. "Giles? Hello?"

Then she spun, listening intently. At night, sound traveled clearly down hallways. It didn't take more than a second to recognize the sounds of a fight, and the location as somewhere nearby.

They're not here, a fight is there, therefore, thus . . .

The thought wasn't halfway finished before she was careening down the hallway, letting her instincts lead her to the science wing.

Xander lay on his back, staring at the ceiling. "Ow?" He tried it again, this time with feeling. "Ow."

"Y'know," a voice said from the hallway, "I'm starting to feel utterly unneeded."

The gang looked up from doctoring their various wounds to see Buffy standing in the hallway, her arms crossed, a mock-petulant look on her face.

"Buffy! We kicked merrow butt!" Willow said triumphantly.

"Looks like some of the kicking was mutual. Everyone okay?"

"Ow," Xander said again, but managed to get up, slowly.

Oz, sitting with his back propped up against a table, managed a weak wave. "Been worse," the musician said. "I'll live to not talk about it."

"That's of the good. Now what happened?"

"As near as I can tell," Giles began, then winced as Willow put a disinfectant on the cut across his forehead. "Sea magic," Giles continued, stopping her from applying a Band-Aid as well, "when performed in terrestrial surroundings, has a, um, a sympathetic magical reaction which creates—"

"What he means," Xander said, "is that our brilliant spellcasters here called them to us."

"Well. In short . . . yes."

"But it was working!" Willow said, determined to find something good in the situation. "The spell, I mean. Until Xander distracted me." She turned to the Watcher, concerned. "Which means, when we substitute sea salt, to give it the extra resonance we need . . ."

Giles nodded. "They'll come more quickly, drawn even more strongly."

"And head straight for Ariel again," Cordelia predicted.

Buffy, following the conversation as best she could, sighed. "Great."

Giles nodded, putting his glasses back on. "Selkies would be a logical food source for merrows in their, ah, natural habitat. And, too, it would appear that they are motivated in part by spite. Ariel's ability to walk on land and live in the sea at will must irk them. We have to assume that they will not simply forget about her."

"So, what," Xander asked, "we stash her somewhere until this is over?"

"No," Buffy said firmly, before Giles could respond. "We don't. We get her out of town, now."

"Buffy, while I'm sure—"

"No, Giles. Maybe it's the magic, maybe they just want a taste of home. But I'm not going to leave her helpless, especially if . . ." Buffy paused for just an instant, then continued firmly, "If something happens to you or Willow, she'd be stuck here forever. Besides," she added when he still hesitated, "I don't like having to work around someone who's completely helpless in a fight."

"Not good to have kids in the line of fire," Xander agreed. "Very distracting."

He suddenly straightened, painfully, his expression cold. Which, on Xander, generally meant only one thing. "Speak of distracting."

Buffy turned as Angel came into the lab. He stopped short, seeing them sprawled in various stages of exhaustion, his gaze flicking over each one and coming to rest on Buffy.

"You're all right!" The vampire amended that quickly to, "You're *all* all right."

"Shouldn't we be?" Xander asked.

Ignoring him, Angel said to Buffy, "I saw the merrows going into the sewers. I would have followed them, to find out where they're denned up, but then I realized they were coming from the school . . ."

And you panicked, Buffy silently finished for him. "We're all right, Angel. All of us. The merrows got the worst of it. But I think this concludes today's game."

"Merrows zero, humans one," Oz said. "I like that score."

"They gonna wait on a rematch?" Xander asked. "Or do we have to go into sudden death overtime? Okay, bad wording, forget I said that."

"They'd go back to the ocean," Angel said. "From what we heard tonight, there's only one group of them, following a leader."

"Like a school of fish?" Willow asked.

Giles nodded. "That would make sense. It would also explain why we haven't been completely overrun, as of yet. If there is only one, ah, school."

"Alpha-pack system," Oz observed. "Infighting's a possibility."

"So the leader will have to keep the rest of the school happy, or risk his position." Buffy thought it through. "That makes sense. So first, they're going to find food, probably fish, something that's not going to fight back too much. Then rest, regain their strength before attacking again."

Giles nodded. "A few hours of sleep would not be amiss for us, either," he suggested. "I don't want to attempt this spell again without a chance to recuperate. And you need to rest as well, Buffy, if you are to convince this school that they don't want to tangle with you."

"Right. So we try again in a couple of hours," Buffy continued, "those of us who . . ." glancing at Angel, "are sort of morning people, anyhow. After everyone's gotten some sleep."

Willow nodded. "I'll get the salt, and then we'll be able to send Ariel home."

Ariel made a yelping, happy sound, and Willow grinned down at her. "You know that word now, huh?"

"I would suggest some additional precautions, however," Giles cut in. "We'll perform the spell itself on the beach. Then, assuming that the merrows do try to come after her, her escape route will be suited to her natural abilities."

"And then I can go after the merrows," Buffy said firmly. "Bad enough having one set of supernatural bottom-feeders hanging around town. Two, and I'll never get downtime."

Angel nodded. "I'll see what I can do about keeping the violence to a minimum tonight. But I can't promise more than a few hours."

"Then that's what we'll take," Buffy said grimly.

CHAPTER 15

"**W**hen I was a kid," Willow said suddenly, "we went on vacation in Maine. Remember, Xander? With my aunt and uncle? I got up one morning to watch the sun rise over the ocean."

"Was it pretty?" Oz asked.

"It was weird. Something not right about the sun coming up over the water, instead of setting on it. Like everything was turned around in the wrong direction."

Oz gave her a swift kiss of reassurance, then another, more lingering, just for the heck of it. The three of them were sitting on the rocks where she had found Ariel, watching the no longer utterly dark sky.

Giles had sent them all home to rest, taking Ariel back to his apartment with him. Oz, Xander, and Willow all ended up at Buffy's house instead of their own, without any real discussion about it. They had meant to shack out there, sort of a group relaxation program, but they had all been too fidgety to actually get any real rest.

Finally, Buffy had called Giles, who seemed relieved as well to get things moving again.

So here they were, outside at dark, in a place where both merrows and vampires were known to frequent.

"Is it just me," Xander said suddenly, "or does this place give everyone else the creeps?"

"A little," Oz agreed.

"No!" Willow said. "Well. A little."

It was the dark, that was all. Dark, and knowing vampires were on the prowl . . . But in about an hour, maybe forty-five minutes, there'd be a gorgeous, vamp-killing sunrise behind them. Or at least there would if the clouds ever got out of the way. Willow cast a last worried look at the sky, then shrugged. If you spent every second of your life worrying about vampires, you wouldn't be able to function at all. And right now, they had something else to do. Other monsters to worry about.

"Hey."

All three of them jumped a little.

"Oh," Willow said. "Hey Angel."

"Everything going all right?" the vampire asked.

"Yeah," Xander muttered. "Just waiting for Buffy and Giles to finish doing . . . whatever it is they're doing."

Angel looked toward the water, where the Watcher and Slayer were talking, and nodded. "Stay alert," he warned. "I found a couple of merrows torn up, a couple of miles away. Might be nothing, but . . ."

"He's another one who's always comforting," Xander said as Angel went down the beach to join Buffy and Giles. "Why doesn't anyone ever give us happy news?"

"Because we live on a Hellmouth?" Oz asked.

"Good point."

Ariel had been curled up at Willow's feet all this time, snoring softly, a cute little burbling noise. Not even Angel's sudden appearance had been enough to wake her.

The selkie had been pretty well traumatized by the fight the night before, instinctively recognizing the merrows for what they were and knowing that she had been in danger of being eaten. But when Willow had finally managed to coax her into letting go of the death grip Ariel had had on the redhead's sweater, the selkie had gone out like a light. Nervous exhaustion, Giles had called it.

And he'd been right: Ariel had woken a few hours later, revived and ready to go. And this morning, it was like the fight had never happened. Animals were like that, living in the moment and not dwelling on stuff that scared them. Willow frowned. But Ariel wasn't an animal. Was she?

When you lived on the Hellmouth, that was a pretty valid question. Was Angel a person? Willow didn't have to think about it. Demon or no, Angel was a person, not a "creature." It had to do with caring, she supposed, and with being aware of what you did and how it affected other people. . . .

Ariel is a person, Willow told herself firmly. A kid-person, but people. More important, she was a friend.

When they'd first gotten Ariel out of Giles's car, she'd started running straight for the ocean, then stopped on her own, sniffed in the ocean's direction, and tugged at her sealskin with a pitiful sadness in her eyes that had made Buffy get down and give her an impromptu hug.

Willow smiled a little at the memory. "Even Buffy's gonna miss her," she said softly. Oz, picking up on her mood, gave her a hug.

"It's good, Ariel's going home."

Willow leaned into the hug for a moment. "I know. I just . . . never had a little sister. Everyone's always been bigger than me."

"I'm not."

Willow giggled at that, and Ariel woke up with a squeaking noise, stretching a little, then turning to look up at the two humans.

"Hey there. Almost ready?" Willow asked her. The selkie must have guessed what she'd said from her tone, because Ariel nodded eagerly, looking down at the waterline.

The water was still blue-black, but now you could see the waves breaking with tiny white foam on the beach. In water that color, it was easy to imagine something lurking below the surface, waiting to drag you in.

"Between merrows and the swim team, I think I won't take up surfing," Xander decided.

"Good choice," Oz agreed.

Giles, Angel, and Buffy were walking down the length of sand, discussing something that involved a great deal of arm waving on the Slayer's part. She was dressed for the occasion in white shorts, sneakers, and a spandex sports top. Willow looked down at her own denim shorts, and felt a momentary, and very familiar resignation.

They're not much, as legs go—too pale, too short, and not exactly what you'd call coordinated, but they're mine. And Oz likes 'em.

Xander had arrived wearing a tee shirt, and swim trunks so astonishingly plaid, nobody could find a comment suitable for them. Oz, on the other hand, stuck to an old pair of jeans and a faded flannel shirt, the sleeves rolled up.

Even Giles had made some small concession to the risk of getting damp, wearing a stiff pair of jeans ironed to a crease and a gray sweater that had definitely seen better days. But his shoes really weren't suited for walking on wet sand.

"You can take the man out of the tweed, but you can't take the tweed out of the man," Xander said, following her gaze.

"Can't imagine Giles in shorts," Oz said.

Xander shuddered. "Please, my trauma plate is already full, thank you."

"Dul abhaite anois?" Ariel asked plaintively.

Willow looked down at the selkie, who was now tugging at her shorts. "Yeah, you'll be going home soon. I hope."

Ariel made a contented sound and settled down again to wait, secure in the knowledge that these humans would be able to help her.

This had better work, Willow thought, her stomach turning butterflies at the idea of another failure. *Is this what it's like to be a parent? I'm not ready for parenting . . .*

"You're freaking, Will," Xander said.

"I am? How can you tell?"

Xander shrugged. "How many years have I watched

you freak over stuff?" he asked rhetorically. "Stop worrying. You know what you're doing."

"Yes, but . . ." She stopped. "No buts. No freaking. I'm calm. I'm capable. I'm . . . Wonder Wiccan!"

Both Oz and Xander grinned. But Ariel suddenly shot to her feet, craning her head to see better. She'd spotted something out in the waves.

"Anois dul?"

Xander winced at the shrill tone. "Geez, Ariel, down a notch, okay? We know you want to get home. Boy, do we ever!"

"Soon, Ariel," Willow said, soothingly. "Soon. Promise."

"Looks like you're on," Oz said, offering her a hand up off the rocks.

Sure enough, Giles was waving at Willow, indicating that she should join them. Taking Ariel by the hand, she left Oz and Xander and walked down to the water's edge. The selkie pulled at her, trying to get her to see whatever it was she had seen.

"I think that we should get started as soon as possible," Giles said. "Ariel's kin are more likely to be nearby at this hour, early morning or twilight being traditional times for magical beings, as well as better feeding times—" Catching a glimpse of Buffy's expression, he added hastily, "The longer we wait, the farther she will have to go to find them again."

"Oh. *Oh.* I hadn't thought of that before. You don't think she'll have any trouble getting back to them, do you?"

"She knows where she is," Buffy reassured Willow. "It'll be like walking home from school. Really. Right, Giles?"

"It should be, yes. Assuming—" He looked at Willow's face, and changed his words midsentence. "Assuming that we are able to get her back into her skin properly."

"Okay," Buffy said, "obvious stuff here: We aren't going to get it done unless we start."

A flicker of amusement crossed Giles's face. "Excellent point. Willow, this time we have more room, so we don't have to abridge the preliminaries."

"A circle! Right! We can draw a ritual circle about us first. You know," Willow added to Buffy, "hold the good stuff in, keep the bad stuff out—well, I'm simplifying, but—"

"Uh-huh," Buffy said. "Easy on the Giles-speak, we got it. Oz and Xander watch the road, Angel and I cover the shoreline, you guys do your stuff, and we get Ariel re-skinned, and on her way home."

Dr. Julian Lee pushed open the library doors cautiously, a plastic-coated field journal in one hand. He didn't feel right about this—it was uncomfortably close to breaking and entering.

But the school is a public building, he reminded himself yet again. *As a law-abiding citizen, I have every right to be here.*

But not at . . . a quick glance at his watch . . . 4:39 A.M., a small voice chided him. Not when you fully intend to riffle through someone's personal belongings.

That the blond girl had been trying to keep him from the small office had been painfully obvious. He hadn't wanted to push it, hadn't known how to get around all of them. But he had to know what they were hiding. Had to find some clue, some piece of evidence that would lead him to the selkie, before more damage was done.

They would understand, once he explained it all to them. They wouldn't be grateful—no one ever was, to have their trust abused, their heart broken—but they'd understand.

"Or not," he said to himself, his voice a harsh whisper in the dead air of the library. He wasn't sure he cared, anymore. The image of Sean's mangled body forced itself back into his mind. If he hadn't been killed by a selkie, then the selkies had definitely led whoever did ashore. They were all dangerous.

Stepping more confidently across the library, he opened the office door and went inside.

An hour later, Lee straightened, stifling a frustrated groan. Books, papers, pamphlets—and nothing he could use! Yes, there were a fair number of books on oceanic research lying unshelved, but those could just as easily be left over from some school project on marine ecology. He didn't want to admit defeat, but another glance at his watch . . . 5 A.M. . . . no, he didn't dare stay here much longer.

Wait. Something under that table . . . a crumpled scrap of paper . . .

Lee scooped it up, heart racing. Too much to hope, and yet . . .

He frowned over the scrawled handwriting. Directions, a familiar sounding street name . . . And then Dr. Lee let out a hiss of disbelief.

"The idiots! The utter, utter idiots!" Lee cried, and ran for the library door.

* * *

Cordelia paused in front of the library door. This was ridiculous. Giles had seemed pretty sure that those merrow-things wouldn't show up anywhere there were a lot of people, something Sunnydale High on a Sunday absolutely did not qualify as. In other words, it was seriously unsafe in the school building—what was she doing here? She should be home, getting the essential sleep she needed to keep her complexion at its prime.

And it's not as if they asked me along. Not that I would have gone, anyway.

But . . . well . . . that kid, the seal-girl, whatever she was, really was cute. And it was kind of sad to think of her stuck here.

Among all those losers.

Right. Besides, the last thing this town needed was *another* supernatural creature taking up permanent residence.

All right, she was here, she'd check. She wasn't going to risk her neck on the beach, but it wouldn't hurt to maybe mind the front office for them. Maybe see if Angel had anything to report, or some weird fax appeared on Giles's desk, telling them the crisis was over, all merrows being recalled to wherever it is they came from.

And besides, if any more of those merrows showed up, she wanted to be where the weapons were.

And maybe they've found a way to ward them off, like shark repellent, or something. God, I hope it doesn't clash with my perfume!

Decided, Cordy started forward—and the library door flew open, nearly hitting her. A man stormed out.

"Dr. Lee! What are you—"

"Where are they?"

Cordelia blinked. "I beg your pardon?"

"Don't play stupid; you're not. Your friends! The selkie!" He grabbed her by the shoulders. "Don't you see? Your friends are in terrible danger!"

Cordy pulled free, smoothing the line of her linen top. "What do you mean, danger?" *Omigod, he knows about the merrows! No, there's no way he could—* "Oh," she said in her most "beyond bored" tone. "Is this all about Ariel again? Because Buffy can hold her own against some kid. Trust me on this."

But she was talking to empty air. Dr. Lee was already storming off at a determined clip, obviously looking for someone else to harass into giving answers.

"Oh, great. If he starts blabbing to everyone . . ."

Cordelia followed, not certain what she would do to stop him, anyway, and watched the man run smack into the two old guys who mopped up the floors and gunk like that. *What are they doing here on a Sunday morning? Right, getting paid. Okay, what am I doing here on a Sunday morning?*

Worrying. Like it or not.

Dr. Lee backed away from the water that had sloshed over one of the pails, and asked them something, his posture seriously intimidating. She caught up with them just in time to hear the guy with some hair left say, seriously defensive, "I don't know what they were doing this time!"

His partner snarled, "Yeah, just once I wish they'd clean up their own mess. I mean, green slime is one thing, but that smell! They call, we come, but the union'd better do something about the conditions here, or we're going to have a walkout."

None of which seemed to satisfy Dr. Lee, who muttered a terse thank you and strode off, Cordelia following on his heels.

"Okay, hang on a second!" she said, finally reaching the end of her patience. If this guy was going to run around, probably make her miss her hair appointment this afternoon, which would take absolutely forever to reschedule, he had better start giving up some information, like *now*. "How, exactly, is Ariel a threat? 'Cause, right now, you're the one who's acting like Looney Tunes Guy. Give me a good reason I shouldn't call the nice men with the white coats and butterfly nets on *you!*"

Lee stared at her, his eyes weirdly blank, like he was totally inside his own head, and not processing what was in front of him.

"The beach," he snapped. "That's where those idiots have gone! Don't they realize the danger's greater closer to *their* element? Sean learned that, too late, and they—they could be torn apart like him, discarded—"

He brushed past her, heading for the main door.

Great. And you just know they're going to blame me if he shows up and ruins everything . . .

Irritated beyond belief, Cordelia went after him.

Buffy dug her heels more firmly into the sand, and watched a small greenish brown crab scuttle along the beach. Guard duty, when there wasn't something actively rushing you, was kind of peaceful, in a boring, rather-be-elsewhere kind of way. About ten feet down the shore, Xander looked almost as bored. Angel and Oz were on the other side of the circle, clearly fascinated by what Willow and Giles were doing.

Yeah, it *was* kind of interesting, she had to admit. If you paid attention to what Giles called the mechanics of magics. The two of them were drawing a circle in the sand, and being Willow and Giles, were making it precisely round by the old "pin in the center, string tied to pin, pencil at end of string" method. Of course, this time, the pin was a piece of driftwood, and the pencil was something that glinted under the cloudy morning sky like silver.

It *was* silver, Buffy realized, that ornate silver letter opener Giles had gotten as an award at some Librarian Convention thingy.

Hey, he finally found a use for it!

"Ariel!" Xander yelled suddenly. "Get back here!"

The selkie had bolted out of the circle while Willow and Giles were preoccupied. She headed for the sea, evading Xander like he was standing still.

"Oh, no you don't. Not yet," Buffy said, catching her by the arm. Ariel whirled to her, eyes wild and unseeing. "Hey, cool it. Chill. You know you can't go back home without the skin."

Angel came up beside her, murmuring what Buffy guessed was an old Irish form of "Chill." His accent was different from Giles's, sounding smoother, but Ariel didn't respond to him.

Giles called impatiently, "Ariel!" He gestured, adding something in his shaky Gaelic that was probably, "Come here or else!" Meekly, the selkie reentered the circle, which Willow, with a sigh, redrew.

"Now?" she asked Giles.

He had an arm around the selkie, holding her in place. "Now," he said firmly.

Willow reached into a little pouch and drew out a

handful of crystals, then raised her hands, palms up, and began the ritual again.

"In your truest form I conjure you."

The glow formed over her palm again, a stronger shade of blue-green this time.

"In your truest form I cleanse you."

In the darkness, the glow looked as though it was sparkling, as though there were tiny bits of mica suspended within the color.

Willow's hands tilted, and the spell ingredients fell onto Ariel's head, the sea salt they used giving off a smell that was the same, but somehow different from the smell of the ocean all around them.

"In your truest form, I release you."

The first part of the spell completed, Willow waited while Giles gently smoothed the mixture onto the skin Ariel held as well. The glow floated from Willow's hands, down to the top of Ariel's head, and waited there.

Ariel held very still, but she was practically quivering in excitement.

Then Giles nodded, and Willow resumed the chant.

"Aegir, look upon your child with favor.

"Aegir, look upon your child with love.

"Release the bonds of human making.

"Release her to the waters.

"Allow her to come home."

The sealskin gave a slight twitch as the glow dissolved into it, and Willow and Giles molded the skin around Ariel's slight form. Then, at a nod from Giles, Willow focused her will and began molding the magical power she could feel still hovering under her hands.

"Fanacht," Giles murmured to the selkie. "Wait. Just a moment longer . . ."

A yell, then a thud—something was happening just outside Willow's range of vision.

"Oh, *argh!*" she said, her concentration broken. She risked a look over her shoulder, still trying to hold the spell together.

Oz and Xander were struggling with a third person, trying to keep him back from the circle. A person who looked horribly familiar . . .

"Dr. Lee!" she cried out in dismay. Then she saw what he was trying to do. "No! Don't!"

Angel swore, and started back toward the circle. Buffy passed him, sprinting across the sand. She saw Oz go down, predicted the arc of Lee's arm that knocked Xander backward, and knew that they weren't going to get there in time.

Giles swept Ariel up in his arms, and Willow stepped in front of both of them, her face twisted as she shouted out some kind of warning—

And then time seemed to slow down as Lee lunged at them. One foot landed right on the line of the circle. Smudging it—and the fragile form of the spell shattered with an almost audible crack. For an instant, all Buffy could hear was the blast of warm wind as all that energy escaped outward. And, carried on that wind, the faint, but very distinct sound of Giles saying, "Oh, bloody hell."

Then time snapped back into focus. Ariel was making some kind of hysterical high-pitched moaning. Willow was flat out on the sand, unconscious; Giles was on his knees beside her. He had a nosebleed, but otherwise seemed okay.

The magical backlash had also hit Lee. He was lying on his butt on the sand, his jaw working but no sound coming out. Then his eyes focused on Ariel, unprotected, and he rolled to his side, struggling to his feet, hunting for something under his sand-covered jacket.

"Buffy, stop him!"

Cordelia? No time to look for her. Quickly gauging distance, Buffy hit Lee with a low flying tackle that would have made any college football scout drool, taking the scientist down again. He landed hard, with a painful *"Ooof!"*

"Don't make me do that again," Buffy said, pinning him. "Much as I would enjoy making you eat a whole lot of sand. Anyone have something of the tying-up sort with them?"

"Emergency Supplies 'R' Us," Xander announced, holding out his hand. Oz, without a word, pulled a pair of handcuffs out of his jeans pocket and handed them to Xander.

"Guaranteed strong enough to hold back wolfboy," Xander said, snapping them around Lee's wrists. "I think they'll do for Doctor Annoying here."

"Good job. Giles? Is Will okay?"

The Watcher looked up from his ministrations. "Yes, she'll be fine. Just a little knocked about."

As if to prove his words, Willow stirred slightly, then tried to sit up.

"Be careful," the Watcher cautioned her. "Backlash is nothing to take lightly."

Willow nodded, then winced. "Anyone catch the number of that truck?"

Ariel stopped her moaning and scurried forward, the skin still molded to her shoulders and sparkling slightly from the aftermath of the spell, to hug the redhead like a favorite toy.

"Yes, Ariel, I'm okay. Oh!" Willow cried, seeing the magical shimmer. "The spell! It got interrupted again!"

Buffy sighed. "So we've got to do it all over again?"

"Right now really wouldn't be a good time," Angel said from behind her. Buffy turned to stare at him—then saw what had caught his attention: a dozen merrows emerging from the surf, the water glistening off their sea-green scales in a way that could have been pretty, but wasn't.

Cordelia, who had been picking her way gingerly along the beach, trying not to ruin another pair of shoes, reached them just in time to hear the exchange. She froze, her face a comic combination of disbelief and resignation.

"Could this get any worse?" she asked.

"Uh, guys . . . ?" Xander pointed to the far end of the beach. "Worse."

Buffy swung around, the hair rising on the back of her neck telling her what she was going to see. Vampires, emerging one at a time from a wide storm drain and dropping down onto the sand. Ten, all looking really, really pissed, their attention focused tightly on the merrows.

Merrows to the left. Vampires to the right. Humans—and vampire, and selkie—in between.

With a whimper, Cordelia summed up the entire situation as only she could:

"You guys are just a *magnet* for the weird, aren't you?"

CHAPTER 16

In times of extreme crisis, there's an instant where you hang suspended in thought, waiting for someone else to make a decision. Unless, of course, you're the Slayer.

"Go!" Buffy shouted, giving the body nearest her—Cordelia—a push. The brunette stumbled forward, nearly losing her footing and a shoe in the sand, then turned around, indignant and scared.

"Go where?" she wailed, gesturing wildly at the vampires rushing at them, cutting them off from the road and the safety of Oz's van.

"Great." The Slayer pulled a stake from the back waistband of her shorts, and held it comfortably in her hand. "Angel, work with me. The rest of you, scatter, do what damage you can without looking too much like targets, okay?"

Even as she spoke, her gaze scanned the beach, looking for something else to use as a weapon—

Oh great. Instead of doing what a sensible guy would—yell at someone to free him—Lee was still lying on the ground, staring in disbelief at the merrows.

Buffy rolled her eyes. "Someone get that idiot out of here!"

"No time," Oz said, his voice steady.

"At least get those cuffs off and give him a weapon!"

Cordelia snatched the keys from Oz and dropped to Dr. Lee's side to unlock the cuffs. He looked at her, blankly, as though unable to remember who she was.

"Terrific." She gave him a good, hard, get-out-of-here shove, then scrambled back to rejoin the group. "I'm not liking this. I mean, I stopped hanging with you losers for a reason. And this was pretty much it."

As she was complaining, Cordelia pulled a stake from the pocketbook still slung over her shoulder, and looked at it. "Think this'll slow down fish guys?"

"It's going to have to," Buffy said, grimly. "Do your best, guys. All we have to do is hold off the vamps until the sun gets high enough to burn them."

"And the merrows?" Xander asked.

"We take care of them on our own," Giles replied grimly, readying his own stake.

And then the two groups were on them.

Okay, this is new, Buffy thought, trying to sweep the legs out from under a merrow, and watching it fall back a pace before charging again. Usually, vampires rushed the nearest warm body, like they couldn't wait to get at your throat.

Well, duh.

But these boys were hanging back, snarling and pacing, like they weren't sure who to attack first, humans or merrows.

Normally, Buffy would be happy to get their attention. Preparatory to dusting them, of course. But Giles was right. Right now, the merrows were the bigger problem.

Mainly 'cause they aren't real picky on who they maul. Like rabid dogs, they're munching just 'cause they're feeling mean.

She set her feet firmly on the damp, packed sand, and used an open-handed slap to fend off a vampire, spinning him into the clutches of a merrow, who chomped down like it was feeding time in the shark tank—then pushed the vamp away, spitting. It looked like Giles was right—again—and the merrows weren't able to tell who was edible and who wasn't until they bit in. *No sense of smell whatsoever. Lucky them, 'cause they smell powerful bad.*

But that meant that they—unlike the vamps—were attacking anything that wasn't them.

"Oz! Watch out!"

Buffy grabbed the merrow heading for her friend, and spun him—her? it?—around.

"Me first, fishsticks."

The merrow snarled and lunged.

This, Giles thought, panting, *was never covered in the handbook. I really need . . . to write an addendum to it someday. Not . . . that the Council will . . . authorize its inclusion—*

He'd snatched up a piece of driftwood and was using it to dual purpose—bashing it over any merrow who got in his way, then reversing it to use as a stake for vampires. It was less than effective, mainly because the drier sand where he was standing created uncertain footing, making it impossible for him to land a firm blow anywhere. *Perhaps I should have listened to Willow when she insisted we attempt the spell barefoot again . . . but I hate the feel of sand between my toes.*

Just as Giles thought that, the sole of his shoe hit a wet patch of sand, and he slid, landing hard on his back, the breath completely knocked out of him. As he struggled just to fill his lungs again, a vampire leaned over him, game face on, and drooling.

"Ariel, come here, uh, *abhus,* now!" Willow ordered, grabbing the selkie and giving the merrow coming their way her best threatening glare.

Unfortunately, her best didn't faze the creature, who had eyes only for the frightened selkie. Its mouth opened, and the teeth flashed forward, then retreated back into the gullet. Willow felt her knees give, like they never had facing down vampires. *Yggggghhhh.* Willow shuddered. *They really are like sharks. Wonder if they eat—no, don't go there, you don't want to think about that!*

Those flat, black eyes showed nothing but hunger, the face gave no indication of what it was thinking, and the way it moved, ungainly but strong, creeped her out completely.

They're inhuman. I mean, more inhuman than non-humans usually are. They're not even humanlike . . .

It took another step closer, and there was a coughing noise, weird, but somehow familiar, coming from the water. Ariel squeaked, her hands scrabbling at the skin that had somehow remained attached to her shoulders despite the flurry of activity. The last remnants of the spell components glittered under her hands, and the skin seemed to . . . expand, flowing and clinging like something alive.

Willow blinked, and reached for the selkie, but Ariel avoided her easily, running into the water, moving faster now than the merrow could on land.

"Ariel!"

Willow caught a flash of an arm lifting out of the waves—no, a flipper! A small, gray seal's flipper, the torpedolike body swimming strongly away from the shore.

It worked! The spell worked! Willow thought in delight. *All it needed was for Ariel to accept it back onto her body!*

The merrow, cheated of its preferred prey, turned back to Willow, its mouth opening again in obvious anticipation of that first bite.

Oh. Uh-oh . . .

Then Oz was beside her, his teeth bared, glaring like he wished it were a full moon, so he could show the merrow who had the really sharp teeth.

He was acting like a fool, Lee snapped at himself, and fools died. *Sean, torn apart like . . . no! Don't think of that!* The pistol, curse it, where was—

His hand closed on it. Teeth bared in a frantic snarl, Lee dragged the weapon out of the folds of his jacket. Now he'd see if these . . . things were mortal enough to die! Hastily, Lee took aim at the nearest of them—

A clawed hand hit his arm with agonizing strength. The gun went flying. Lee scrambled after it, but other clawed hands caught him by both arms. Even though he struggled with all his strength, digging his feet into the sand, he was dragged relentlessly toward the waves. Toward the demons' home. Toward death—

"No! I'm not ready yet, you!"

A wave caught him in the face, and Lee broke off, choking. It was hopeless. He was going to die in the ocean . . . ironic, amusingly ironic, after all . . .

Something slammed into the creatures holding him and they lost their grip. A seal? No! A selkie! That was surely a selkie! *Maelen?* rushed through Lee's stunned brain.

No, impossible. And the selkie hadn't saved him, just knocked him out of the way so it could fight the other demon. No matter, no matter, it gave him a chance to get free.

Lee scrambled frantically out of the water. Time to analyze what had just happened some other time.

Assuming he lived long enough for there to *be* some other time!

Angel was wary of the merrows, remembering all too well what the touch of their claws had done to his system. All right, he'd use that memory, that anger and frustration at not being able to control his own body or strike back at these invaders. Feeling his features shift, he lunged at one, fingers digging under scales and ripping a few off. Green blood flowed thickly, clotting almost instantly.

Slow blooded, Angel noted even as he went in for another strike. *Heavy on the coagulants. No wonder they taste so awful.*

Slaying was generally a lonely business. Just you, and the uglies. Sure, sometimes there were a whole bunch of them, and sometimes you had to take them all on in the middle of a crowded mall, but one thing you rarely had to worry about was bumping into someone during the fight!

But then Buffy was out of the melee, her backswing getting lots of open space behind it, before she brought her stake down and dusted a particularly persistent vamp in cowboy boots and fringed denim.

"And it's another victory for the fashion police!"

Buffy barely managed to finish her obligatory quip before a sudden heavy weight on her back sent her staggering forward. Hard, cold hands grabbed her upper arms, and heavy, dank breath raised gooseflesh on her neck.

"You are so not going to get a date unless you start brushing your teeth," Buffy said, combining a backward-moving elbow with a drop-the-shoulder-and-twist movement that should have had her free, and her assailant on the sand, gasping for air. Or water. Or whatever it was these things breathed.

Instead, she found herself lying on her side, sand in her face, with the merrow still firmly attached to her with its claws.

Claws. Oh, no . . .

She could feel it now, the cold slow seep of numbness in her arms. *Not good. Not good at all.* Slayer healing should shake off the worst of it quickly. Should, though, being the operative term here.

Desperate to get this thing off her, Buffy tried to roll a little, to see if she could improve her leverage.

The slap of cold water in her face was a shock.

Oh. Mistake.

Their tussling had moved them far enough down the

beach that they were now in the water. The merrow's element. But, on the plus side, she was so cold now, the numbness didn't seem so bad.

Before Buffy could react, the merrow started dragging her into deeper water, the current moving them down the beach, away from the others.

And then the merrow dove under a wave, taking her with it . . .

The water was all around her, blue-green, murky and cold . . . It flooded her lungs, seared her brain, and cold, webby hands grabbed hold of her, dragging her down, pulling her away from the air, away from life . . .

Then the pressure was released, and Buffy shot to the surface, gasping for air, and looking around wildly for the merrow.

The cold brush of something in the water beside her made her look down. The merrow, its scaled neck lolling at an impossible angle, floated on its back next to her.

Buffy looked up and saw Angel standing in the hip-deep water across from her.

"So much for your saltwater theory," she said, gasping a little for breath.

"I took the risk."

He extended a hand, and she hauled on it, making a face as she felt chilly air on wet clothes, making her shiver despite the warmth a good fight built up. "Yeah, I—"

Suddenly they were under attack again, this time by three merrows who had obviously decided that anything in the water was fair game.

Buffy went after the nearest, then realized that she'd lost hold of her stake somewhere in the water.

Uh-oh . . .

The merrow grinned, showing its weird double rows of teeth, and moved forward. Angel had his hands full with the other two, trying to take them down without getting slashed by their claws. Farther up on the beach, she could see her friends still fighting vampires—was that Giles down on the sand?

Stop it! Think about the here and now, worry about them later.

First, there has to be a later.

The vampire looming over him suddenly exploded into a sparkling of dust, and Giles blinked up at Xander Harris.

"Save the thanks for later, G-man. Cordy needs some help."

The Watcher nodded, kicking off his shoes and getting to his feet. The sand felt distinctly unpleasant through his socks, but his footing was much more secure.

Cordelia was a dozen yards farther up the beach, caught between three vampires and a merrow. Lee, a few yards behind her, was clearly in shock, unable to defend himself.

Giles grabbed the driftwood and ran toward them, dodging a merrow and a vampire locked in a bitter choking match.

Xander whirled and nearly collided with a merrow. As it snatched at him, he dodged, slipped on the sand, and went flat on his back, propelling the merrow neatly over his head. As it crashed down on the beach, Xander scrambled up, thinking, *Hey, neat, that actually worked!*

But the merrow wasn't out of the fight. Xander gave a yelp of pain as sharp claws clamped down on the calf of his left leg.

"Hey, let go!"

He was struggling across the sand, dragging the creature like a stubborn dog.

"Stupid fish, let go before I kick your teeth in!"

He stumbled, caught up a rock, and hit the merrow over the head. "Let go of me! I said—let go!"

With a grunt, it went limp, and Xander staggered free. But . . . he couldn't . . .

"I hate fish," Xander said, and collapsed.

Somehow, Angel had managed to work his way back to the main fight, standing ankle-deep in the saltwater, trying to keep his balance as the surf rolled around him, and enemies rushed at him. Vampires and merrows both, coming at him from different angles, each with a completely different style of fighting. He was holding his own, but for how long?

And how long did he have before sunrise? The demon inside him wasn't worried—long enough. Good news for him, bad for his human friends. He had to get to the beach, help them.

Ashes scattered on the water surface, and Angel spared the time before dealing with the next opponent to look over his shoulder, scanning the water one last time. *Where is Buffy?*

Fighting in water, Buffy discovered, was exhausting. Now she knew why aqua-aerobics was so popular— you got twice the workout when your hardest kick had only half the impact. Great for your heart rate—lousy for beating up on the bad guys. None of her usual moves was working, and the one time she did try to kick—useless. *Time to improvise.*

Diving under an oncoming wavelet, she forced her eyes open against the saltwater and scanned the sandy bottom, looking for something that could be used as a weapon. But the water was so murky, she couldn't see anything other than gray.

She was almost out of breath, swimming to avoid the vampire thrashing around looking for her, when the quick pass of something to her left made her jerk away in reflex. The sleek shape passed—*what was that?*—but something fell from it, water bubbles rising in its trail.

Reflexively, Buffy caught the object as she rushed to the surface, even her Slayer-enhanced lungs gasping for air.

The vampire was in her face the moment she surfaced, and Buffy slashed out with the object, only after the fact realizing that she was holding a piece of driftwood, about the size of her hand, rough and splintery, although water-soaked. The edge had been carved or—no, chewed—making it semi-sharp, almost like a pencil point.

"Gotcha!" Buffy said in satisfaction, and drove the wood into the vampire's heart with all the force she could muster.

The dust fell on the water in pretty patterns, which Buffy barely had time to admire before a pair of hard, scaled hands grabbed her around the ankles and dragged her back underwater.

Back to her nightmare . . .

Even on a sunny day, the water would have been

dark. With the cloud cover still obscuring any possible light, the darkness was a terrifying thing. And it didn't help that her brain immediately starting playing the theme from *Jaws*. Frantically struggling, Buffy managed to break free for a moment, gasping in a desperate breath, thinking, *I've got to get off this drowning kick!*

She heard an odd, sing-song barking noise, like the grown-up version of Ariel's whining, and realized that what helped her before was a selkie. *Ariel? Or maybe one of her missing parents?* Didn't matter. Suddenly inspired, Buffy shouted out "Help me, underwater!"

She was dragged under again by hard, scaled hands, but managed to push off with one foot against a merrow's face, and surfaced again, gasping. "We're trying to help, but this is your home, too!" she shouted, hoping the selkies were still within range, and listening.

Nothing. Nada. Struggling, Buffy was pulled underwater yet again. *So much for good intentions.* Desperate for air, lungs aching till she could have screamed—if that wouldn't have meant drowning—she could feel her dream coming true . . .

One last struggle . . . a brief, precious moment back at the surface, a quick, wonderful gulp of air—

And the weird barking song all at once slid into a beautiful, haunting melody.

Weird, all right. Buffy could feel the power of it tingling through the water, almost like electricity. The remaining merrows broke away, the barking noises a taunt, a reminder that there was easier prey to be found in deeper water, food that didn't kick and stake and kill, leaving Buffy floundering and gasping in sweet, sweet lungfuls of air, in shoulder-deep water.

Ok. No collapse. Not yet.

She paused, trying to force her water-logged brain into processing it all. *The seal-guys are taking care of merrows, luring them back out into deep sea. Where they all belong. That of the good. But meantime, no rest for the water-logged . . .*

Heh. Driftwood. Grabbing up an improvised stake, Buffy went after the last of the water-logged vampires. Hardly a challenge. No breath left for quips, either.

Not caring. So *not caring.*

But once she emerged, there were no vampires left to fight. Buffy grinned. Her gang had done her proud. *Way to go,* she thought wearily, then staggered up the beach to where the gang, and a shamefaced Dr. Lee, were tending to Xander. "Just a bad clawing," she heard Giles assure them all.

"Good," Xander said, and went flat.

"Good idea," Buffy agreed, and sat down. So did the others. Exhausted, they all sat and caught their breath. Only Angel remained standing, his clothing completely waterlogged, his hair plastered to his scalp, looking like a drowned rat. *Okay,* Buffy amended, *a tall, extremely hot rat, but drowned nonetheless.*

And, to her surprise, she found that she could think of drowning, even joke about it, without so much as a flicker of a twitch. *Yay me,* she thought. *Nothing like a little trauma to fix a phobia.*

"You're going to be okay?" Angel asked the group.

"Just peachy," Buffy assured him. "Go, get out of here before the sun rises."

He cast another glance at them, then at the beach,

where only traces of green blood being absorbed into the scuffed-up sand indicated anything had happened.

"Go," Giles said wearily. Angel looked at the Watcher, nodded, and was gone.

Buffy lay back down on the sand and stared up at the sky, which was beginning to shade into predawn pink.

"Anyone else for hot fudge sundaes for breakfast?"

CHAPTER 17

The next morning was clear, the sky a pale blue; the kind of day when nothing, it would seem, could go wrong.

Rupert Giles distrusted those kinds of days on basic principle. But Sunnydale was a surprising place, so it was with a cautious optimism that he opened the library on his normal noncrisis schedule, and looked around.

No disasters appeared to have struck overnight, except, perhaps, the fact that once again someone had left a can of root beer on the counter.

With a *"tsk,"* he placed it in the recycling bin, and started to reshelve the books which had piled up in the past week, glad of the soothing regularity of the task. It gave his mind a chance to go over the recent events, to try to put them into some kind of order before committing them to history in his journal.

Yesterday, after the battle, had ended up a rather

quiet day—surprising, considering how it had begun. Fortunately, the effects of the neurotoxin had worn off swiftly, and none of the injuries had required an Emergency Room visit.

For which I am thankful! I am running out of excuses to give, not that the emergency technicians believe them, anyway.

Were it not for the fact that he, more often than not, was the worst off, Giles suspected he would have been called in long ago to account for the teens' injuries.

Although, he mused, it was rapidly becoming obvious that the town of Sunnydale as a whole did indeed suffer from what Xander referred to as Total Cluelessitis. Otherwise, it would no doubt be a ghost town, in the figurative if not the literal sense of the phrase.

Buffy had gone on patrol last night and reported a total lack of activity. It would appear that the vampire community was still recovering.

He hoped it would take them quite some time.

There was the sudden sound of the door swinging open, and the clack of heels on the tile—ah yes, Cordelia Chase.

"So," she began, then stopped.

Giles waited. Surely, Cordelia would speak her mind soon enough. It had never taken her very long before.

"Ariel got home okay?" she said at last. "I mean, she didn't show up on your doorstep or anything last night?"

Giles shook his head, surprisingly touched by the fact that Cordelia had bothered to inquire.

"No. Willow heard from Dr. Lee earlier this morning. He has been tracking the coastline, and the herd which was in our waters yesterday has gone back out to sea. I assume that Ariel was with them."

"Good. And what are we going to do about Dr. Lee?"

The Watcher smiled, a bit grimly. "Apparently, things with large teeth are sufficient to distract him. He's been quite helpful in getting further information about what is lurking off our shores."

"Oh." Cordelia shifted, leaning against the counter and playing with the straps of her pocketbook nervously. "I guess he's all over the selkie-hunting thing, then, huh?"

"Actually, no. He's still quite convinced that Ariel abandoned us in the middle of the fight. Even Buffy's avowals that it was a selkie who aided her, it appears, will not change his mind about the essential soullessness of the selkie race, and their threat to humans."

"Oh," she said again.

Giles rather thought he knew where this was going. "You don't get over that sort of betrayal overnight," he said almost casually, putting several books down on the cart and picking up another, carefully not watching Cordelia's face. "Love removed so suddenly seems to demand an equally strong emotion to replace it."

"Like hatred."

"Like hatred," Giles agreed. "Or fear."

"Does it ever go away?"

He did look at her then, his eyes sad, but his mouth curved in a slightly hopeful smile. "It fades. And, when you're ready to move on, it is often replaced with . . . regret. And finally, perhaps, with a memory of the better times, untainted by the bad."

"Oh. So—maybe one day Dr. Lee will be able to remember the good times with his wife?"

"Someday," Giles said. "When he's ready."

The bell rang, indicating a class change, and she gathered her books. "I, ah, gotta go." But in the doorway, Cordy paused, and said quickly over her shoulder, "Thanks."

She nearly collided with Buffy. "Hey."

The startled Buffy answered, "Hey," and hurried into the library. "What did you say to her, Giles? She *smiled* at me. I mean, a real smile, not like Cordelia at all."

"And you?"

"Well, yeah, I smiled back at her."

So did Giles. "Good."

Buffy waited, but he didn't say anything else on the subject.

"Right. We're moving on. You said you had a book that would teach me more about dreams and stuff?"

Giles nodded, indicating a small stack of books on the table.

"I should have insisted that you learn dream recognition before this all began. Had you been more confident in your deconstruction of the images, perhaps we could have avoided—" he paused, seeing something in her expression. "There's something else?"

Buffy nodded, walking forward slowly to pick up the top book on her pile and flip through it idly. "It's Will. I mean, she's glad about Ariel going home, and all that. But, well, I think she still feels bad about Ariel's not saying good-bye, or anything. Like she just abandoned us, the minute she could go home.

"Not that Willow would ever say that, you know, or even think it—but you can see it on her face."

Giles nodded. "Ariel was a young girl, long separated from her family, suddenly given a chance to return. It is understandable that she forget her newer friends under those conditions. Willow will understand that, once she's given it some thought. And you?"

Buffy shot him a look, then shrugged. "You're asking if I'm over my wig about her? I guess. Okay, so maybe it was the whole sea-thing going on, and maybe—maybe!—there was a little jealousy going on, too. But I think maybe I'm never going to be totally comfortable around things that aren't human."

"That may be," he agreed. "Certainly, you will always be aware of their differences. But there are no lasting ill effects from the dreams? No lingering discomfort?"

Buffy grinned then, the picture of carefree youth. "Nope. Not an emotional scar to be seen. As for Ariel, I'm just glad we got her off safely—signed, sealed, and delivered, so to speak."

Giles groaned at the joke. "Out," and he pointed to the door. "Now."

Laughing, a book tucked carefully under her arm, Buffy obeyed.

About the Authors

Laura Anne Gilman's short fiction has appeared in the magazines *Amazing Stories* and *Dreams of Decadence*, and the anthologies *Urban Nightmares, Lammas Night,* and *Blood Thirst: 100 Years of Vampire Fiction.* The co-author of *Buffy the Vampire Slayer: Visitors* with Josepha Sherman, she also co-edited the anthologies *OtherWere: Stories of Transformation,* and the forthcoming *Treachery & Treason.* She lives in northern New Jersey with her husband, Peter, and cat, Pandora (who was the inspiration for *Deep Water*'s "Ariel"), and can be reached on the web at www.sff.net/people/lauraanne.gilman.

Josepha Sherman is a fantasy writer and folklorist whose books include the *Highlander* novel *The Captive Soul;* the *Xena* book *Xena: All I Need to Know I Learned from the Warrior Princess, by Gabriell, as Translated by Josepha Sherman;* and the folklore volume *Merlin's Kin: World Tales of the Hero Magician.* She is a member of the Author's Guild, SFWA, and the American Folklore Society. She is probably the first folklorist to give a paper on the changing role of the Klingon at the American Folklore Society. It goes without saying that she is a fan of *Buffy!* She can be reached at *www.sff.net/people/Josepha.Sherman.*

Everyone's got his demons....

ANGEL™

If it takes an eternity, he will make amends.

❖

Original stories based on the
TV show created by Joss Whedon
& David Greenwalt

Available from Pocket Pulse
Published by Pocket Books

. . . A GIRL BORN
WITHOUT THE FEAR GENE

FEARLESS™

A NEW SERIES BY
FRANCINE PASCAL

A TITLE AVAILABLE EVERY MONTH

From Pocket Pulse
Published by Pocket Books